Also by Larry Niven:
    THE MAGIC GOES AWAY

The Patchwork Girl

by Larry Niven

Illustrated by Fernando

THE PATCHWORK GIRL

Copyright © 1980 by Larry Niven

Illustrations copyright © 1980 by Fernando

An ACE Book
A Division of Charter Communications Inc.
A GROSSET & DUNLAP COMPANY
360 Park Avenue South
New York, New York 10010

First Ace printing: April 1980

2 4 6 8 0 9 7 5 3 1
Manufactured in the United States of America

Contents

To my father. RIP.

1.

City of Mirrors

We fell east-to-west, dipping toward the Moon in the usual, shallow, graceful arc. Our pilot had turned off the cabin lights to give us a view. The sun set as we fell. I peered past Tom Reinecke and let my eyes adjust.

It was black below. There wasn't even Earthlight; the "new" Earth was a slender sliver in the eastern sky. The black shadows of mountains emerged from the western horizon and came toward us.

Reinecke had fallen silent.

That was a new development. Tom Reinecke had been trying to interview me even before we left Outback Field, Australia. Thus:

What was it like, out there among the flying mountains? Had I really killed an organlegger by using psychic powers? As a man of many cultures—Kansas farm boy, seven years mining the asteroids, five years in the United Nations Police —didn't I consider myself the ideal delegate to a Conference to Review Lunar Law? How did I feel about what liberals called "the organ bank problem"? Would I demonstrate my imaginary arm, please? Et cetera.

I'd admitted to being a liberal, and denied being the solar system's foremost expert on lunar law, inasmuch as I'd never been on the Moon. Beyond that, I'd managed to get him talking about himself. He'd never stopped.

The flatlander reporter was a small, rounded man in his early twenties, brown-haired and smooth-shaven. Born in Australia, schooled in England, he'd never been in space. He'd gone from journalism school straight into a job with the BBC. He'd told me about himself at length. This young, and he was on his way to the Moon! To witness deliberations that could affect all of future history! He seemed eager and innocent. I wondered how many older, more experienced newstapers had turned down his assignment.

Now, suddenly, he was quiet. More: he was leaving fingerprints in the hard plastic chair arms.

The black shadows of the D'Alembert Mountains were coming right at us: broken teeth in a godling's jaw, ready to chew us up.

We passed low over the mountains, almost between the peaks, and continued to fall. Now the land was chewed by new and old meteorite craters. Light ahead of us became a long line of lighted windows, the west face of Hovestraydt City. Slowing, we passed north of the city and curved around. The city was a square border of light, and peculiar reflections flashed from within the border: mostly greens, some reds, yellows, browns.

The ship hovered and settled east of the city, at the edge of Grimalde's rim wall. No dust sprayed around us as we touched down. Too many ships had landed here over the last century. The dust was all gone.

Tom Reinecke let go of his chair arms and resumed breathing. He forced a smile. "Thrill a minute."

"Hey, you weren't *worried*, were you? You can't even *imagine* the *real* problems with making this kind of landing."

"What? What do you mean? I—"

I laughed. "Relax, I was kidding. People have been landing on the Moon for a hundred and fifty years, and they've only had two accidents."

We fought politely for room to struggle into our pressure suits.

If Garner had given me a little more warning I would have had a skintight pressure suit made at the taxpayers' expense. But skintight suits have to be carefully fitted, and that takes time. Luke Garner had given me just ten days to get ready. I'd spent the time on research. I was half certain that Garner had picked someone else for the job, and that he or she had died or gotten sick or pregnant.

Be that as it may: I had bought an inflated suit on the expense account. The other passengers, reporters and Conference delegates, were also getting into inflated suits.

Half a dozen people, lunies and Belters, waited to greet us when we climbed down from the airlock. I could see fairly well into the bubble helmets. Taffy wasn't among them. I recognised people I'd seen only on phone screens. And a familiar voice: cheerful, cordial, mildly accented.

"Welcome to Hovestraydt City," said the voice of Mayor Hove Watson. "You've arrived near dinner time by the city clocks. I hope to show you around a bit before you begin your work tomorrow." I had no trouble picking him out of the crowd: a lunie over eight feet tall, with thinning blond hair and a cordial smile showing through his helmet, and a flowering ash tree on his chest. "You've already been assigned rooms, and—before I forget—the city computer's command name is *Chiron*. It will be keyed to your voice. Shall we postpone introductions until we can get into shirtsleeves?" He turned to lead the way.

So Taffy hadn't made it. I wondered if she'd left a message ... and how long it would be before I reached a phone.

We trooped toward the lights a few hundred yards away. No moondust softened our footfalls. My first look at the Moon, and I wasn't seeing much. Black night around us and a glare of light from the city. But the sky was the sky I remembered, the Belter's sky, stars by the hundred thousand, so hard and bright you could reach up and feel their heat. I lagged behind to get the full effect. It was like homecoming.

We were Belters and flatlanders and lunies, and there was no problem telling us apart.

All the flatlanders, including me, were wearing inflated suits in bright primary colors. They hampered movement, made us clumsy. Even I was having trouble.

I'd talked to the other United Nations delegates just before the flight. Jabez Stone was a cross between tall black Watusi and long-jawed white New Englander. He'd been a prosecution lawyer before he went into politics. He represented the General Assembly. Octavia Budrys of the Security Council had very white skin and very black hair. She was overweight, but with the muscle tension to carry it well. You sensed their awareness of their own power. On Earth they had walked like rulers. Here—

Their dignity suffered. Budrys bounced like a big rubber ball. Stone fought the lower gravity with a kind of shuffle. They veered from side to side and into each other. I heard their panting in my earphones.

The Belters found their stride easily. Through the bubble helmets you saw Belter crests on both men and women: hair running in a strip from forehead to nape of neck, the scalp shaved on both sides. They wore silvered cloaks against the cold of lunar night. Under the cloaks were skintights: membranous elastic cloth that would pass sweat and that fitted like a coat of paint.

Paintings glowed across their chests and bellies. A Belter's pressure suit is his real home, and he will spend a fortune on a good torso painting. The brawny redheaded woman wearing the gold of the Belt police had to be Marion Shaeffer. Her torso showed an eagle-clawed dragon stooping on a tiger. A broad-shouldered black-haired man, Chris Penzler, wore a copy of a Bonnie Dalzell griffon, the one in the New York Metropolitan: mostly gold and bronze, with a cloudy Earth clutched in one claw.

I had abandoned a Belter suit when I returned to Earth. The chest painting showed a great brass-bound door opening on a lush world with two suns. I missed it.

The lunies wore skintights, but they would never be taken for Belters. They stood seven and eight feet tall. Their suits were in bright monochrome colors, to stand out against a bright and confusing lunar background. Their chest paintings were smaller, and generally not as good, and tended to feature one dominant color ... as Mayor Watson's ash tree painting was mostly green. The lunies hardly walked; they flew in shallow arcs, effortlessly, and it was beautiful to watch.

One hundred and fifty-seven years after the first landing on the Earth's Moon, you could almost believe that mankind was dividing into different species. We were three branches of humanity, trooping toward the lights.

Most of Hovestraydt City was underground. That square of light was only the top of it. Three sides of the square were living quarters; I had seen light spilling through windows. But the whole east face of the city was given over to the mirror works.

We passed telescope mirrors in the polishing stage, with mobile screens to shield them. Silicate ore stood in impressively tall conical heaps. Spindly lunies in skintights and silver cloaks stopped work to watch us pass. They didn't smile.

Under a roof that had rock and moondust piled high atop it for meteor protection, a wide stretch of the east face was open to vacuum. Here were big, fragile paraboloids, and lightweight telescope assemblies for Belter ships; widgetry for polishing and silvering mirrors, and more widgetry for measuring their curvature; garage space for wide-wheeled motorcycles, and bubble-topped busses, and special trucks to carry lenses and radar reflectors. There were more lunies at work. I'd expected to see amusement at the way we walked; but they weren't amused. Was that resentment I saw within the bubble helmets?

I could guess what was bothering them. The Conference.

Tom Reinecke veered away to peer through a glass wall. I followed him. Lunie workmen were looking this way; I was afraid he'd get in trouble.

He was looking down through thick glass. Beyond and below, an assembly line was birthing acre-sized sheets of silvered fabric, rolling the fabric into tubes with the silvering on the inside, sealing the ends, and folding it into relatively tiny packets.

"City of Mirrors," Tom said reflectively.

"You know it," said a woman's voice. Belt accent, specifically Confinement Asteroid. I found her at my shoulder. Within the bubble helmet she was young and pretty, and very black: Watusi genes, skin blackened further by the unfiltered sunlight of space. She was almost as tall as a lunie, but the style of her suit made her a Belter. I liked her torso painting. Against the pastel glow of the Veil Nebula, a slender woman's silhouette showed in uttermost black, save for two glowing greenish-white eyes.

"City of Mirrors. There are Hove City mirrors everywhere in space, everywhere you look," she told us. "Not just telescopes. You know what they're doing down there? Those are solar reflectors. They're shipped out flat. We inflate them. Then we spray foam plastic struts on them. They don't have to be strong. We cut them up and get cylindrical mirrors for solar power."

"I've been a Belt miner," I said.

She looked at me curiously. "I'm Desiree Porter, newstaper for the Vesta Beam."

"Tom Reinecke, BBC."

"Gil Hamilton, ARM delegate, and we're being abandoned."

Her teeth flashed like lightning in a black sky. "Gil the Arm! I know about you!" She looked where I was pointing, and added, "Yah, we'll talk later. I want to interview you."

We jumped to join the last of the line as it cycled through the airlock.

We crowded into different elevators and rejoined on the sixth level, the dining facility. Mayor Watson again took the lead. You couldn't get lost, following Mayor Watson. Eight feet two inches tall, topped with ash blond hair and a nose like the prow of a ship, and a smile that showed a good many very white teeth.

By now we were talking away like old friends ... some of us, anyway. Clay and Budrys, the other UN delegates, still had to keep all their attention on their feet; and they still bounded too high. And I got my first look at the Garden, but I didn't get a chance to study it till we were seated.

We were three delegates from the United Nations, three from the Belt, and four representing the Moon itself, plus Porter and Reinecke, and Mayor Watson as our host.

The dining hall was crowded and the noise level was high. Mayor Watson was out of earshot, at the other end of the table. He'd tried to mix us up a little. The reporters seemed to be interviewing each other, and liking what they learned. I found myself between Chris Penzler, Fourth Speaker for the Belt, and a Tycho Dome official named

Bertha Carmody. She was intimidating: seven feet three, with a spreading crown of tightly curled white hair, a strong jaw and a penetrating voice.

The Garden ran vertically through Hovestraydt City: a great pit lined with ledges. A bedspring-shaped ramp ran up the center, and narrower ramps fed into it at all levels, including this one. The plants that covered the ledges were crops, but that didn't keep them from being pretty. Melons hung along one ledge. A ledge of glossy green ground cover turned out to be raspberries and strawberries. There were ledges of ripe corn and unripe wheat and tomatoes. The orange and lemon trees lower down were blooming.

Chris Penzler caught me gaping. "Tomorrow," he said. "You're seeing it by sunlamps now. By daylight it's quite beautiful."

I was surprised. "Didn't you just get here? Like the rest of us?"

"No, I've been here a week. And I was here at the first Conference twenty years ago. They've dug the city deeper since. The Garden too." Penzler was a burly Belter nearing fifty. His immense, sloping shoulders made his otherwise acceptable legs look spindly. He must have spent much of his life in free fall. His Belter crest was still black, but it had thinned on top to leave an isolated tuft on his forehead. His brows formed a single furry black ridge across his eyes.

I said, "I'd think direct sunlight would kill plants."

When Penzler started to answer, Bertha Carmody rode him down. "Direct sunlight would. The convex mirrors on the roof thin the sunlight and spread it about. We set more mirrors at the bottom of the pit, and the sides, to direct the sunlight everywhere. Every city on the Moon uses essentially the same system." She refrained from adding that I should have done my research before I came; but I could almost hear her thinking it.

Lunies were bringing us plates and food. Special service. The other diners were all getting their own from a ledge, buffet style. I plied my chopsticks. They had splayed ends, and they worked better than a spoon and fork in low gravity. Dinner was mostly vegetables, roughly Chinese in approach, and quite good. When I found chicken meat I turned again to the Garden. There were birds flying between the ledges, though most had settled for the night. Pigeons and chickens. Chickens fly very well in low gravity.

A dark-haired young man was talking to the Mayor.

I admit to being abnormally curious; but how could I help but stare? The kid was the Mayor's height, a couple of inches over eight feet, and even thinner. Age hard to estimate; say eighteen plus-or-minus three. They looked like Tolkien elves. Elvish king and elvish prince in well-mannered disagreement. They were not enjoying their inaudible conversation, and they cut it short as quickly as possible.

My eyes followed the kid back to his table. A table for two, across the width of the Garden. His companion was an extraordinarily beautiful woman ... a flatlander. As he sat down the woman darted a look of pure poison in our direction.

For an instant our eyes locked.

It was Naomi Horne!

She knew me. Our eyes held ... and we broke the lock and went back to eating. It had been fourteen years since I last felt the urge to talk to Naomi Horne, and I didn't have it now.

We ended with melon and coffee. Most of us were heading for the elevator when Chris Penzler took my arm. "Look down into the Garden," he said.

I did. It was another nine stories to the bottom; I counted. A tree was growing down there. Its top was only two levels below us. The ramp spiraled down around the trunk.

"That redwood," Chris said, "was planted when Hovestraydt City was first occupied. It's much taller now than it was when I first came. They transplant it whenever they dig the Garden deeper."

We turned away. I asked, "What's it going to be like, this Conference?"

"Less hectic than the last one, I hope. Twenty years ago we carved out the general body of law that now rules the

Moon." He frowned. "I have my doubts. Some of the lunar citizenry think we are meddling in their internal affairs."

"They've got a point."

"Of course they do. We face other opportunities for embarrassment, too. The holding tanks were expensive. Worse, the lunar delegates are in a position to claim that they serve no useful purpose."

"Chris, I'm a last-minute replacement. I only had ten days to bone up."

"Ah. Well, the first Conference was twenty years ago. It wasn't easy finding compromises between three ways of life. You flatlanders saw no reason why lunar law shouldn't send all felons to the organ banks. Belt law is considerably more lenient. The death penalty is so damned *permanent*. Suppose it turns out that you broke up the wrong person?"

"I know about the holding tanks," I said.

"They were our most important point of compromise."

"Six months, isn't it? The convict stays in suspended animation for six months before they break him up. If the conviction is reversed, he's revived."

"That's right. What you may not know," Chris said, "is that no convict has been revived in the past twenty years. The Moon had to pay half the cost of the holding tanks ... well, we could have made them pay the whole bill. And there were some bugs in the prototypes. We know four convicts died and had to be broken up at once, and half the organs were lost."

We crowded into the elevator with the rest. We lowered our voices. "And all for nothing?"

"By lunie standards, yes. But how diligently were the rights of the convicts guarded? Well. As I say, the Conference may be more hectic than one would hope."

We all got off on zero level. I gathered that few lunies wanted to live on the surface. These rooms were mostly for transients. I left Penzler at his door and walked two down to my own.

2.

View Through a Window

Wherever you go in space, shirtsleeve environments tend to be cramped. My room was bigger than I expected. There was a bed, narrow but long, and a table with four collapsed chairs, and a tub. There was a phone screen, and I made for that.

Taffy wasn't in, but she'd left a message. She wore a paper surgical coverall and sounded a bit breathless. "Gil, I can't meet you. You'll get in about ten minutes after I go on duty. I get off at the usual ungodly hour, in this case 0600, city time. Can you meet me for breakfast? Ten past six, in oh-fifty-three, in the north face on zero level. There's room service. Isn't Garner lovely?"

The picture smiled enchantingly, and froze. Chiron asked, "Will there be an answer, sir?" and beeped.

I was still feeling ruffled and mean. I had to force the eager smile. "Chiron, message. Ten past six, your room. I'll come to you by Earthlight, though Hell should bar the way." Called off the phone and lost the smile.

Lucas Garner was in his hundred-and-seventies. He had a face to scare babies. He was confined to a wheelchair because half his spinal cord had died of old age. He delegated a lot of authority, but he led the United Nations Police—still called the Amalgamated Regional Militia, the ARM—and he was my boss. And for getting me this chance to see Taffy again after two and a half months of separation ... yeah, Garner was lovely.

Taffy and I had been roommates for three years when she got this chance to practice surgery on the Moon. Exchange program. It wasn't something she could turn down: too useful to her career, and too much fun. They'd been rotating her among the lunar cities. She'd been in Hovestraydt City almost two weeks now.

She'd taken to dating a lunie GP, McCavity by name. I refuse to admit that that irritated me; but the way her schedule had messed up our first meeting did. So did the thought of the Conference meeting, tomorrow at nine thirty. I'd heard angry voices at dinner. Clay and Budrys hadn't mastered the art of walking yet, and it would affect their tempers.

And my own feet kept getting tangled.

What I needed was a soak in a hot bath.

The bathtub was strange. It was right out in the open, next to the bed, with a view of the phone screen and the picture window. It wasn't long, but it stood four feet high, with a rim that curved inward, and the back rose six feet before curving over. The overflow drain was only half-way up. I started water running, then watched, fascinated. The water looked like it was actively trying to escape.

I tried some commands. The door lock, the closet lock, the lights all responded to my voice and the *Chiron* command. The water closet lock was manual.

Presently the bath was full to the overflow line. I got in, carefully, and stretched out. The water dipped in a meniscus around me, reluctant to wet me, until I added soap.

I played with the water, jetting it up between my hands, watching it slowly rise and slowly fall back. I stopped when I'd got too much on the ceiling and it was dripping back in fat globules. I was feeling a lot better. I found tiny holes under me and tried calling, "Chiron, activate spa." Water and air bubbles churned around me, battering muscles strained by low gravity walking.

The phone rang.

Taffy? I called, "Chiron, spa off. Answer phone." The screen rotated to face me. It was Naomi.

In low gravity her long, soft golden hair floated around her with every motion. Her cheekbones were high in an oval face. She was made up in recent flatlander style, so that her blue eyes were patterns on the wings of a great gaudy butterfly. Her mouth was small, her face just a touch fuller than I remembered.

Her body was still athletic, tall and slender by flatlander standards. Her dress was soft blue, and it clung to her as if by static electricity. She'd changed in fourteen years, but not much ... not enough.

It was unrequited love, and it had lasted half of a spring and all of summer, until the day I invested my scanty for-

tune to loft myself from Earth and outfit myself as an asteroid miner. The scar on my heart had healed over. Of course it had. But I'd known her across a crowded restaurant. At that distance a stranger would barely have known her for a flatlander.

She smiled, a bit nervously. "Gil. I saw you at dinner. Do you remember me?"

"Naomi Horne. Hi."

"Hi. Naomi Mitchison now. What are you doing on the Moon, Gil?" She sounded a bit breathless. She'd always talked like that, eager to get the words out, as if someone might interrupt.

"Conference to Review Lunar Law. I represent the ARM. How about you?"

"I'm sightseeing. My life kind of came apart awhile back ... I remember now, you were on the news. You'd caught some kind of organlegging kingpin—"

"Anubis."

"Right." Pause. "Can we meet for a drink?"

I'd already made that decision. "Sure, we'll squeeze it in somewhere. I don't know just how busy I'll be. See, I actually came here following my ex-roommate. She's a surgeon on loan to the hospital here. Between Taffy's weird hours and the Conference itself—"

"You're likely to meet yourself in the halls. Yes, I see."

"But I'll call you. Hey, who was your date?"

She laughed. "Alan Watson. He's Mayor Hove's son. I don't think the Mayor approves of his dating a flatlander. Lunies are a bit prudish, don't you think?"

"I haven't had a chance to find out. I can't seem to guess a lunie's age—"

"He's nineteen." She was teasing me a little. "They can't tell our ages either. He's nice, Gil, but he's very serious. Like you were."

"Uh huh. Okay, I'll leave a message if I get loose. Would you object to a foursome? For dinner?"

"Sounds good. Chiron, phone off."

I scowled at the blank screen. I had an erection under the water. She still affected me that way. She couldn't have seen it; the camera angle was wrong. "Chiron, activate spa," I said, and the evidence disappeared in bubbles.

Strange. She thought it was *funny* that a man would want to take her to bed. I'd told myself that, fourteen years ago, but I don't think I believed it. I'd thought it was me.

And, strange: Naomi was clearly relieved when I told her about Taffy. So why had she called? Not because she wanted a date!

I stood up in the tub. A half-inch sheath of water came up with me. I scraped most of it back into the tub with the edges of my hands, then toweled myself off from the top down.

The picture window was jet black but for a small glowing triangle.

"Chiron, lights off," I said. Blind, I took a chair and waited for my eyes to adjust. Gradually the view took form. Starlight glazed the battered lands to the west. Dawn was creeping down the highest peak. A floating mountain seemed to flame among the stars. I watched until I saw a second peak come alight. Then I set the alarm and went to bed.

"Phone call, Mr. Hamilton," a neuter voice was saying. "Phone call, Mr. Hamilton. Phone c—"

"Chiron, answer phone!" I had trouble sitting up. There was a broad strap across my chest; I unfastened it. The phone screen showed Tom Reinecke, and Desiree Porter bending low to put her face next to his. "It better be good," I said.

"It's not good, but it's not dull," Tom said. "Would an ARM be interested in the attempted murder of a Conference delegate?"

I rubbed my eyes. "He would. Who?"

"Chris Penzler. Fourth Speaker for the Belt."

"Does nudity offend you?"

Desiree laughed. Tom said, "No. It bothers lunies."

"Okay. Tell me about it." I got up and started putting clothes on while they talked. The screen and camera rotated to follow me.

"We're next to Penzler's room," Desiree said. "At least Tom is. The walls are thin. We heard a kind of godawful slosh-*thump* and sort of a feeble scream. We went and pounded on his door. No answer. I stayed while Tom phoned the lunie cops."

"I phoned them, then Marion Sheaffer," Tom said. "She's a Belter too, the goldskin delegate. Okay, she showed up, then the cops, and they talked the door open. Penzler was face up in his bathtub with a big hole in his chest. He was still alive when they kicked us out."

"My fault," Desiree said. "I took some pictures."

I had my clothes on and hair brushed. "I'll be there. Chiron, phone off."

Penzler's door was closed. Desiree said, "They've got my camera. Can you get it back for me?"

"I'll try." I pushed the bell.

"And the pictures?"

"I'll try."

Marion Shaeffer was in uniform. She was my height, muscular, with broad shoulders and heavy breasts. Her ancestors would have been strong farm wives. Her deep tan ended sharply at the throat. "Come in, Hamilton, but stay out of the way. It's not really your territory."

"Nor yours."

"He's one of my people."

Chris Penzler's room was much like mine. It seemed crowded. Three of the six people present were lunies, and that made a difference. I got an impression of too many elbows flashing in my personal space. One was a redheaded, heavily freckled lunie policeman in orange marked with black. He was working the phone. The blond man in informal pajamas was just watching, and he was Mayor Watson himself. The third was a doctor, and he was working on Penzler.

They'd wheeled up a mobile autodoc, a heavy, dauntingly complex machine armed with scalpels, surgical lasers, clamps, hypos, suction tubes, sensor fingers ending in tiny bristles, all mounted on a huge adjustable stand. That took up room too. The lunie was hard at work monitoring the keyboard and screen set into the 'doc, sometimes typing rapid-fire commands with his long, fragile-looking fingers.

Penzler was on his back on the bed. The bed was wet with water and blood. A pressure bottle was feeding blood into Penzler's arm; you can't use gravity feed on the Moon. We watched as the autodoc finished spraying foam over Penzler, until it covered him from his chin to his navel.

I swore under my breath, but I couldn't really claim they should have waited for me.

"Here." Marion Shaeffer elbowed me in the ribs and handed me three holograms. "The reporters took pictures. Good thing. Nobody else had a camera."

The first picture showed Penzler on the bed. His whole chest was an ugly deep red, beginning to blister around the edges, but burned worse than that in the center. White and black showed where a charred hole had been burned deep into the bone of the sternum, an inch wide and an inch deep. The wound must have been sponged out before the picture was taken.

The second holo showed him face up in bloody bathwater. The wounds were the same, and he looked dead.

The third was a shot through the picture window, taken over the rim of the tub.

"I don't get this," I said.

Penzler turned his head a bare minimum and looked at me with suffering eyes. "Laser. Shot me through the window."

"Most laser wounds don't spread like this. The wound would be narrower and deeper ... wouldn't it, doctor?"

The doctor jerked his chin down and up without looking around. But Penzler made a strong effort to face me. The doctor stopped him with a hand on his shoulder.

"Laser. I saw. Stood up in the tub. Saw someone out there on the Moon." Penzler stopped to pant a bit, then, "Red light. Blast bounced me back in the water. Laser!"

"Chris, did you see only one person?"

"Yah," he grunted.

Mayor Watson spoke for the first time. "How? It's night out there. How could you see anything?"

"I saw him," Penzler said thickly. "Three hundred, four hundred meters. Past the big tilted rock."

I asked, "What was he? Lunie, Belter, flatlander? What was he wearing?"

"Couldn't see. It happened too fast. I stood up, I looked out, then *flash*. I thought ... for a second ... I couldn't tell."

"Let him rest now," the doctor said.

Nuts. Penzler should have seen that much. Not that it would prove anything. A Belter could wear a pressure suit. A flatlander could get a skintight made, though you'd expect to find records. A lunie ... well, there exist short lunies; shorter than, for instance, Desiree Porter, who was a Belter.

I stepped past the tub to reach the window. The tub was still full of pink water. Penzler would have bled to death, or drowned, if Tom and Desiree hadn't acted so quickly.

I looked out on the Moon.

Dawn had crawled down the peaks to touch their bases. Most of the lowlands were still puddles of black, and the shadow of Hovestraydt City seemed to stretch away forever. Out of the city's shadow, a hundred and ninety yards away to left of center, was a massive monolith that could be Penzler's "big tilted rock". It was the shape of an

elongated egg, and smooth. Perhaps the surface had been polished by the blast that made Grimalde Crater.

"It's a wonder he saw anything at all," I said. "Why didn't the killer just keep to the shadows? The sun wasn't up yet."

Nobody answered. Penzler was unconscious now. The doctor patted his shoulder and said, "Three or four days, the foam will start to peel off. He can come to me then and I'll remove it. It'll be longer than that before the bone heals, though."

He turned to us. "It was close. A few minutes later and he would have been dead. The beam charred part of the sternum and cooked tissue underneath. I had to replace parts of his esophagus, the *superior vena cava,* some mesentery ... scrape out the charred bone and fill it full of pins ... it was a mess. On Earth he wouldn't move for a week, and then he'd want a wheelchair."

I asked, "Suppose the beam had been three inches lower?"

"Heart cooked, pleural cavity ruptured. Are you Gil Hamilton?" He stuck out a hand. "I believe we have a friend in common. I'm Harry McCavity."

I smiled and shook his hand (carefully, fighting temptation; those long fingers did look fragile). My thoughts were only mildly malicious. Doctor McCavity wasn't with Taffy either tonight.

McCavity had fluffy brown hair and a nose like an eagle's beak. He was short for a lunie, but he still looked like he'd grown up on a stretch rack. Only lunies look like that. Belters raise their children in great bubble-structures spun up to an Earth gravity, places like Confinement and Farmer's Asteroid. McCavity was handsome in an elvish, eery fashion. In no way did he seem freakish.

"Weird," he said. "Do you know what saved his life?" He jerked a long thumb at the bathtub. "He stood up, and a lot of water came up with him. The laser beam plowed into the water. Live steam exploded all over his chest, but it saved his life too. The water spread the beam. It didn't go deep enough to kill him right away. The steam explosion threw him back in the tub, so the killer didn't get a second chance."

I remembered how the water had sheathed me when I stood up in the tub. But— "Would it spread that much? Mayor, could the glass in the window cut some of the light?"

The Mayor shook his head. "He said red light. The window wouldn't stop red light. It filters raw sunlight, but mainly in the blue and ultraviolet and X-ray range."

"We ought to let him sleep," McCavity said. We followed him out.

The corridor was high because lunies are high, and wide for a touch of luxury. Windows looked down into the Garden.

The newstapers were waiting. Desiree Porter confronted Marion Shaeffer. "I'd like my camera back, please."

Shaeffer handed over the bulky, two-handed instrument.

"And my holos?"

She jerked a thumb at the freckled, seven-foot-high lunie cop. "Captain Jefferson's got 'em. They're evidence."

Tom Reinecke confronted Harry McCavity. "Doctor, what is Chris Penzler's condition? Is it murder or attempted murder?"

McCavity smiled. "Attempted. He'll be all right. He should rest tomorrow, but I think he'll be well enough to attend the Conference afterward. Mayor, are you through with me? I'm tired."

Captain Jefferson said, "We'll need your evidence on the nature of the wound, but not just now."

McCavity waved and departed, leaping down the corridor like a frog, both feet pushing at the floor at the same time.

Mayor Hove Watson watched him go. His face was

puzzled, thoughtful. He came to himself with a start. "What about it, Gil? What would the ARM be doing, if this were Los Angeles?"

"Nothing. Murder isn't ARM business, unless it involves organlegging or esoteric technology. I've investigated some murders, though. Mainly we'd try to track the weapon."

"We'll do that. Chris said red light. That probably means it was a message laser, and they're guarded. The police use them for weapons as well as senders."

"Guarded how?" I noticed that both newstapers were listening quietly.

"The locks are controlled by the same computer that operates your own apartment, including the door lock. It's a different program, of course."

"Okay. What about opportunity? There was a killer out on the Moon. He can't stay out forever."

Mayor Hove turned to the lunie cop. "We have no secrets, Jefferson."

"Yessir. We were lucky," Jefferson told us. "First, it's city night *and* lunar night. Well, pre-dawn. Most of the population is in their apartments, and we can account for some of the rest. One flatlander tourist is out on the Moon, and nobody else as far as we can tell. We're checking the night shift at the mirror works. If it were daylight we'd have hundreds of suspects. Second, the Watchbird Two satellite rose ten minutes ago. I've had the projection room made ready for us."

"Very good." Mayor Hove rubbed his eyes. "Proceed with your investigations, Captain. Detectives Hamilton and Shaeffer may accompany you if they wish. The reporters ... well, use your own judgment." He dropped his voice to tell me, "I thought it politic to let Mr. Penzler see me concerned in his behalf; but I'd be of no more use here..." And he jumped off down the corridor.

The rest of us followed Jefferson to an elevator.

3.

The Projection Room

The projection room was a big box let into Levels Six and Seven, underground, in the south side. The police had a projection going when we arrived. They were wading knee deep in miniature lunar landscape.

I think the newstapers were jolted. I know I was.

Jefferson beamed at us. "The Watchbird Two satellite is just over us now. It sends us a picture and we project it in real time."

He waded out into the Moon, and we followed, thigh deep and a hundred feet tall. I could see my feet through the flat stone surface of Grimalde Crater, if I concentrated.

Dawn had fully arrived. The sun glared on the eastern horizon, not far below the crescent Earth. The crater-pocked landscape west of us was all glaring ridges and black shadows. Hovestraydt City was a doll house. Tiny figures in bright orange skintights with police insignia were leaving an airlock in the south face, on the road that led across the badlands to the Belt Trading Post.

Someone was walking toward them down the middle of the road. I bent close above the doll-figure, looking for details. An inflated suit, sky blue, shorter than the approaching lunie cops. Blond hair in the bubble helmet.

I heard a satisfied, "Ah." When I turned, Marion Shaeffer added, "I was pretty sure it would be a flatlander."

Penzler's room would be second from the end in the west face. I picked it out, then traced a line to a tilted rock like an elongated egg. Past that point it was mostly shadows. I saw nobody anywhere in that whole stretch of moonscape, save for a sky blue suit and four orange ones, converging.

"We seem to have only one suspect," Captain Jefferson said. "Even a puffer wouldn't take a killer out of range that fast."

Shaeffer asked, "Puffer?"

"Basically two wheels and a motor and a saddle. We use them a lot."

"Ah. What about a spacecraft?"

"We checked, of course. The only spacecraft in the vicinity came nowhere near here."

I was thinking along different lines. "What's a message laser look like? Our little blue suspect doesn't seem to be carrying anything."

"We'd see it. A message laser is about yay long—" Jefferson's hands were a yard, or meter, apart. "—and masses nine kilos."

"Well, those shadows could hide anything. Mind if I feel around in there? I might turn up the weapon."

Tom and Desiree grinned at each other. Shaeffer stared. Jefferson said, "What? What did you say?"

The newstapers laughed outright. Desiree said, "He's Gil the Arm. Haven't you ever heard of Gil the Arm?"

"He's got an imaginary arm," Tom added.

With impressive restraint Jefferson said, "Oh?"

"Combination of psychic powers," I told him. "I lost my arm to a meteor, asteroid mining. Eventually I came back to Earth and got it replaced from the organ banks. But before that happened I found out that I've got a couple of the recognised psi powers. Esper sense: I can feel around inside a closed box, and reach through a wall and feel out the wiring behind it. Psychokinesis: I can move things with my mind, if they're not too heavy. But it's all limited by my imagination. As if I had a ghost arm and hand."

I didn't bother to add that psychic powers are notoriously undependable. What gave me confidence, this time, was that I was already trying it: running my imaginary hand lightly over the smooth surface of the Grimalde plain, feeling its texture—cooled magma, cracked everywhere, the cracks filled by moondust—then plunging my hand in and running the ghostly rock between my fingers like water. Hard rock here; pools of moondust in the rough land beyond Grimalde's rim wall; here beneath the dust, an oxygen tank split down the middle by internal pressure. "It'd help if I knew what a message laser looks like," I added.

Captain Jefferson used his belt phone to summon someone with a message laser. "While we're waiting," he said,

"maybe you'd like to feel around in here?" He patted at the southeast corner of the hologram city.

I reached into the wall. I found a small room, cramped, lined with racks. The only door felt thick, massive. It opened into the mirror works, in vacuum. I found varied equipment on the racks: armored inflated suits, personal jet packs, a heavy two-handed cutting torch. I described what I was finding. My audience could be expected to include skeptics.

And I tried not to think about what was actually happening: my own disembodied sense of touch reaching through rock walls to roam through a locked room seven floors above me. If I stopped believing, it couldn't happen.

The racks held a score of things like bulky rifles.

I pinched one between my thumb and two fingers. Rifle-stock frame, compact excitation barrel, tingle of battery power, and a scope just big enough to feel as a bump. The message laser felt both light and heavy: no mass at all, yet impossible to move.

A cop came in carrying the real thing. I held it in my hands, and ran my imaginary hand over it, then through it. There was a dimmer switch, and a cord that would plug into a pressure suit's microphone.

You could talk with it. I wouldn't have been surprised either way. Calling a deadly police weapon a "message laser" could have been no more than good public relations.

I waded west into the choppy cratered land our would-be-killer must have fired from. The newstapers and lunie cops were watching me intently. God knows what they expected to see. I swept my imaginary hand back and forth through the landscape, like sifting intangible sand. The killer might well have dumped his weapon into a dust pool. He might equally well be hiding in one of those shadows, I thought, with a stock of air tanks and spare batteries. I sifted them.

Pools and lakes of shadow felt very cold, and showed nothing, though I could feel the shapes of the rocks. Once I felt something like a twelve-foot artillery shell smashed against a crater rim. I asked Jefferson about it. He said it was probably from the rescue attempt after the Blowout eighteen years ago. It would have held water or air.

There was a high ridge, a crater wall. I felt around in the shadows behind it. The killer couldn't have been placed further back than this. The ridge would have blocked him, and it was already further than Chris Penzler's "three hundred, four hundred meters".

I turned and went back over the same territory again. By now I was feeling foolish. No laser, no hidden killer, and the beginning of a headache.

The neon orange dolls had collected the blue doll and were going through the airlock. I waded back to where the others waited. I said, "I quit."

The others didn't hide their disappointment. Then Desiree brightened and said, "You'll have to testify, won't you? No weapon and no other suspect."

"I guess I will. Let's go see who they've got."

The desk sergeant was a lunie woman with rounded oriental features and big boobs.

Forgive me! Later I got to know Laura Drury fairly well; but I was seeing her for the first time, and I admit I stared. On her spare, attenuated frame her attractive, ample breasts became her dominant feature. You don't picture a Tolkien elf that way.

We stopped in the doorway, not wanting to interfere. Sergeant Drury asked, "Is this your first visit to the Moon, Ms. Mitchison?"

And I went numb.

Naomi's eyes flicked to us and away. It was the desk sergeant who concerned her. She knew she was in trouble, and it made her voice brittle. "No, I was at the museum in Mare Tranquilitatis four years ago."

"Did you see much of the Moon then?"

The shock was getting through to me. One suspect had been in position to fire through Chris Penzler's window. I

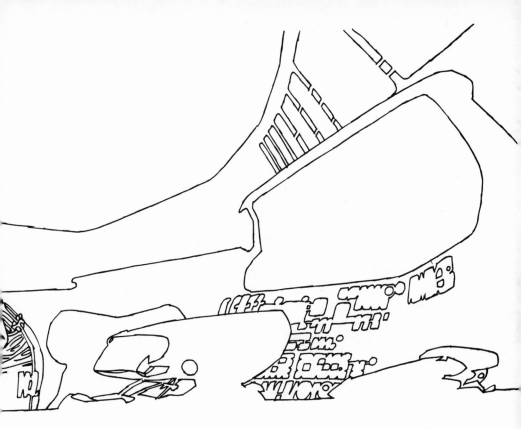

would have to testify that nobody was hiding out there in the shadows. I'd eliminated everyone but Naomi.

It was insane. What could Naomi have to do with Chris Penzler? But I remembered a vindictive glare directed toward our dinner table last night. For Penzler?

Her golden hair was still rumpled from the pressure suit helmet. The rest of the suit was still on her. The big gaudy blue butterfly still covered her eyelids. She sat on the forward edge of a web chair. "I only stayed a week that time," she said. "I . . . was in the mood for a dead world, but I was wrapped up in myself too. My husband and my little girl had just died. I guess I spent most of my time staring out the window of my room."

"You left Hovestraydt City alone this evening," the desk sergeant said. "You've been out four and a half hours. For a tourist that is reckless. Did you keep to known paths?"

"No, I played tourist. I wandered. I spent some time on the big road, but I ducked into the shadows and the craters every so often. Why not? I couldn't get lost. I could see Earth."

"Did you take a signal laser?"

"No. Nobody told me to. Have I broken some fool regulation, sergeant?"

The lunie woman's lips twitched. "In a manner of speaking. You are accused of having stationed yourself several hundred meters west of the city; of having located Fourth Speaker Chris Penzler's window, and kept watch until he stood up in his bathtub, at which time you fired a signal laser into his chest. Did you do that?"

Naomi was amazed, then horrified . . . or she was a fine actress. "No. Why would I?" She turned. "Gil? Are you in on this?"

"Only as an observer," I half-lied. Marion was looking at me with distrust. Clearly the suspect knew me.

The desk sergeant asked, "Ms. Mitchison? Do you *know* Chris Penzler?"

"I used to. He's a Belter. My husband and I met him on Earth, almost five years ago. He was negotiating with the UN about some kind of jurisdictional problem. Is he dead?"

"No. He is badly injured."

"And you're really accusing me of attempted murder? With a message laser?"

"We are, yes."

"But . . . I don't have any reason. I don't have a message laser either. Why me?" Her eyes flicked about the room: a butterfly fluttering against a window. "Gil?"

I flinched. "I'm not in this. It's not my jurisdiction."

"Gil, is attempted murder an organ bank crime? On the Moon?"

Sergeant Drury answered for me. "Why would we give a clumsy killer a second chance?"

"You can refuse to answer questions," I said.

Naomi shook her head. "That's all right. But . . . is that a news camera?"

Jefferson crooked his finger at Tom and Desiree. The

newstapers looked at each other and somehow agreed that resistance would be futile. They followed Jefferson out.

The desk sergeant's eyes flicked to Marion. "Who might you be?"

"Marion Shaeffer, Captain, Belt police. The man who was shot is a Belt citizen."

Drury's eyes questioned me, and I answered. "Gil Hamilton, operative, ARM, here for the Conference. I know Ms. Mitchison. I'd like to stay."

"Have you any suggestions?"

"Yes. Naomi, one problem is that we can't find anyone else who could have been in the right place. You were.

You've said you didn't shoot Chris—"

"With *what?*"

"Who cares? If you're not our clumsy killer, then you're our only witness. Did you see anything unusual out there?"

She thought about it. "I'm handicapped, Gil. I don't know the Moon, and it was night. I didn't see anyone else."

"Did you drop anything, or brush against anything, or break anything? Is there some way we could tell just where you were?"

"You could examine my suit." Hostility was creeping into her voice.

"Oh, we'll do that. We'd also like to examine your route. You'd have to lead us. We can't make you do that."

"Gil, can I get some sleep first?"

I looked at the Sergeant Drury, who said, "Of course. You may find it easier when the sun's higher." She sent Naomi off with another cop.

"We've got men out there," she said briskly. "There won't be anyone tampering with evidence. What do you know about her?"

"I haven't seen Naomi in ten years. I wouldn't have said she was the killer type. When you take her outside, may I go along?"

"We'll alert you. And you, Ms. Shaeffer."

"Thanks. Make that Marion."

"Okay. I'm Laura Drury. Make it Laura."

We waited for the elevators. Marion said, "Gil, what do you consider the killer type?"

"Yeah, that's a hard one, isn't it? But Naomi strikes me as more the murder *victim* type."

"What do you mean?"

She sounded like she was questioning a suspect. I put it down to habit. I said, "Once upon a time I might have killed her myself. Naomi has a way of ... inviting a pass, then slapping the passer down hard. I really think she gets a charge out of leaving a man horny and frustrated. This isn't just subjective, Marion. I've heard other guys talk about it. Still ... it was ten years ago, and she got married somewhere in there, and had a little girl. So. Your guess is as good as mine."

The elevator came. We got in. Marion said, "I don't have to guess. She was the only one out there, and she's a flatlander."

"So?"

She smiled. "The wound was too high. Eight, nine centimeters above the heart. Why?"

"The rim of the tub was too high."

"Right. Now, there aren't any tubs in the Belt, except in the bubble worlds. A flatlander wouldn't expect a lunie bathtub to stand so tall. When it came time to make her move, Naomi couldn't see Penzler's heart. She just took her best shot."

I shook my head. "A lunie would know how tall the tub was, but he wouldn't expect Penzler to be so short."

"He must have *seen* Penzler—"

"Sure, and Naomi's seen lunie bathtubs, too." While she was mulling that, I added, "Maybe it was a Belter. You said it yourself, the only tubs in the Belt are in the bubble worlds. You spin those for an Earth gravity. Belt bathtubs are just like Earth's."

Marion grinned. "Got me."

"And we're still missing the main point. Why didn't the killer just wait till Penzler got out of the tub? If it was Naomi, she'd already been waiting most of four hours."

"Now, that is a *damn* good question," Marion said. And we parted on that note, her to her room, me to mine. I could catch two or three hours on my back before 0610.

At exactly 0610 I rang Taffy's doorbell.

"Gil! Are you alone?"

The long stretch of hall was quite empty. "At this hour, what sane man would be up?"

"Chiron, open door."

I walked in. And she was already in flight! I leaned far forward to catch her weight, and managed not to bounce back into the hall. We took a long time over our first kiss. Tasting each other. By and by I noticed that she was wearing a surgeon's paper coverall. Those things are intended to be used only once.

"Can I rip this off you?"

"Be my guest."

I tore it off in handfuls, with sound effects: the roar of an unendurably frustrated male. The paper was tough. A lunie couldn't have done it. I swept her in my arms and leapt for the bed, and bounced off again. Pulled my own clothes off more sedately, moved back to the bed, and had some trouble.

She whispered in my ear. "Let me dominate, okay? I've had some practice. The missionary position doesn't work at all."

"What do I have to know?"

Partly she told me, partly she showed me. We had to use our muscles to keep us together; gravity wouldn't help. We bounced. We spent considerable time above the bed. Taffy told me not to worry about falling off, and I didn't. Old and accustomed partners danced a new dance, with Taffy leading.

We rested. Then I made love to her standing up, with Taffy's strong legs wrapped around my hips, one arm out to clutch the edge of the tub. In lunar gravity that position is almost restful. And I studied her face, joyful, glowing, familiar.

We rested again. Sweat stayed where it was; it wouldn't drip. Taffy stirred in my arms and asked, "Hungry?"

"Yes!"

There was a tray on the table. Scrambled eggs, chicken wings, toast, coffee. "It may have cooled off," she said. "It had to get here before you did. Otherwise we'd have to be dressed."

We ate. I asked, "What is it with lunies? I keep hearing remarks. It's the kind of thing you'd expect in the eighteenth century, with social diseases and no contraceptives."

She nodded and swallowed and said, "Harry tried to explain it to me. People have been living on the Moon for a hundred and twenty years or so, but even eighty years ago there were only a few hundred. Human beings haven't really adapted biologically to having children in low gravity. Maybe someday, but for now . . . they marry early and have two or three children and never use a contraceptive at all. Two or three children and a dozen or two dozen pregnancies that don't come to term. The children are precious. It's very important who the father is."

"Uh *huh*."

"That's the official position. But there are contraceptives, and *somebody's* buying them. And long engagements are normal, and children born seven or eight months after the ceremony are also normal. I'd guess they try each other out, just like we do, but one at a time, and what they're looking for is fertility, not compatibility. And they don't talk about even that."

"Except Harry."

She nodded. "Harry likes flatlander women. Society kind of frowns on that, but Harry's too good a doctor to be fired." She grinned at me. "That's his story. He's actually damned good. And he's sterile, guaranteed. There are a fair number of men like that, and women too. They're in a special position. Not really considered a threat, if you follow."

I wanted to know more about that relationship. I tried an oblique approach. "Would you recommend that I take a lunie lover?"

She didn't smile. "Don't fail to seduce a lunie, Gil. What I mean is, *don't fail*. Don't ask unless the answer is *yes*. In fact—" Now she smiled. "Don't ask. You can let yourself be seduced. Everyone knows flatlanders are easy."

"Are we?"

"Sure. Now, would you like to meet Harry McCavity? Is

that what you were getting at? You'd like him, and he doesn't consider you a threat. Quite the reverse."

"What?"

"You're a good cover. You and I are roommates of long standing. Hove City society would really prefer that Harry keep his relationships purely social."

"Oh. Okay, I'd like to meet him socially. I met him officially last night. He was repairing a hole in a Belt delegate." I told her about Penzler.

She didn't like it. "Gil, if someone's shooting at offworld Conference delegates, shouldn't you start wearing a mirror vest? And me too?"

"Not to worry. They've got a suspect."

"That's a relief. The right suspect?"

"She was the only one out there." I discovered that I didn't want to talk to Taffy about Naomi. "They'll be expecting to call me in my room. And I need some sleep. When shall we twain meet again?"

"It looks like Thursday, same time, unless someone changes my schedule again."

"Same time. Lord."

"I thought you were used to my funny hours. Look, I'll leave you a message if it looks like we can get together with Harry. Lunch or dinner, okay?"

"Okay."

It was nine when I reached my room. I called the Mayor's office, got his secretary, and was told that the Conference had been postponed for that day, but the conference room would be open for informal discussions.

Interesting. Chris was that important? But two other delegates had been up late into the night, and others could be suffering from time lag. I was just as glad they'd called it off.

I slept till noon. Then Laura Drury called. She was just going off duty, and a team of lunie police were leaving with Naomi in ten minutes.

4.

The Cratered Lands

I got into my suit in a hell of a hurry, then stopped and made myself go through the checkout routine. I was long out of practice. I reached the south face airlock and found the rest of the party still in sight on the road. I bounced after them.

There were seven of us: Naomi, Marion Shaeffer, me, and

four tall lunie cops. The freckled rehead was Jefferson. The
face above the tallest of the orange suits was also familiar.
I'd seen him talking to the Mayor last night at dinner.

"Alan Watson?"

"Yes, that's right. You're one of the Conference delegates—"

"Gil Hamilton. ARM." We shook gloves. He was a thin young man with straight black hair, a narrow nose, thick shaggy eyebrows, blunt-fingered hands as strong as mine. He couldn't make himself smile. Frightened for Naomi? The smallish painting on his chest showed an esoteric spacecraft nearing the North America nebula, all in reds and blacks.

We set off, Naomi leading. The road west was a trade road; it sometimes carried heavy equipment, up to the size of a damaged spacecraft. It was broad and smooth, but not straight. Follow it far enough and you would reach the Belt Trading Post.

We had come four or five hundred yards, without much conversation, when Naomi said, "I turned off here. I wanted to climb that rock."

She was pointing at a faceted lump a considerable distance away. It was the tallest point around. I had first seen it glowing in darkness, lit by imminent dawn, when I looked out my window last night.

We followed Naomi toward it. Marion asked, "Did you climb it?"

"Yes."

The sun was only six degrees up the sky. We walked in shadow most of the time. It would have been like wading through ink, but for our headlamps. The footing was chancy. Naomi stumbled as often as I did, more often than the lunies. Marion had trouble too.

She stopped Naomi at one point, where our only route of approach would round a spur of black volcanic glass. "Okay, what's around this turn?"

"I don't know," Naomi said. "It was dark, it was all different. I'm not even sure this is the way I came."

The peak was a thousand feet high and not particularly steep. It would give a good view of Hove City, I thought; but we were north of where Chris Penzler had spotted his assassin. A cop directed Naomi to climb it.

She wasn't exactly agile, in unfamiliar gravity, with the inflated suit restricting her movements. But she didn't have any trouble till she was three hundred feet up. Then she started yelping. She came down dangerously fast.

"It's hot!" she complained. "It burned me right through the suit!"

"Where?" Alan Watson demanded.

"My chest and arms. It's okay now, I think, but I can't climb it in daylight. Shall I try the other side?"

Marion said, "No, skip it. Where next?"

Naomi led us south. I wondered if we would learn anything this way. Whether or not she was lying, her answer would be the same: it was dark, I don't know the Moon, this probably isn't the way I came. Tentatively, she had lied already. When I'd climbed out of my tub, the peak was sunlit for the upper hundred feet. Why had she tried to climb the sunlit side today, if she'd had the chance to learn better last night?

Of course she could have started earlier yesterday . . . and climbed in total darkness. I didn't like that either.

And I hated where she was leading us.

This was familiar territory. I had sifted it in miniature, felt its contours with my imaginary hand. I half-remembered landmarks large or strange; and so, it seemed, did Naomi.

Like a hill-sized boulder that had split nicely down the middle, leaving flat planes uppermost. Naomi described it before we reached it. She pointed out one half of the split monolith and said, "I climbed up on that one. I lay on my back and looked at the stars, and sometimes at Hove City. More than half the windows were dark by then. There was nice backlighting from behind, from the spaceport and the mirror works."

She moved to climb up on it, but Marion yanked her back. The orange-clad cops searched with headlamps and powerful flashlights, for bootscrapes, footprints, anything Naomi might have dropped. When they gave up on the sides, Watson and Jefferson reached the top in one leap and searched that. Slanted sunlight made the lamps unnecessary.

Marion jumped up and joined them. She balanced on boot-toes and fingertips and searched with her face two inches from the rock.

"Nothing," she said. "Are you sure you were in this territory?"

"I was right up there on that rock!"

Marion looked satisfied; Jefferson looked grim; Alan Watson had a haunted look. I climbed up after them, knowing.

It was roomy and almost flat. It would be a good place to stretch out and watch stars. I looked toward the city, and Chris Penzler's "tilted rock" was almost in line-of-sight, assuming I had the right rock. I could look right into Chris's window, around four hundred yards away. The sun made me squint. But at night that window would make a fine shooting gallery.

I thought it over for a few seconds. Then I said, "Hamilton speaking. I'd like to try a couple of things, if nobody has any objection. First, I'd like to test fire a message laser."

I used Jefferson's. He showed me how to hook the transceiver cable into my helmet mike, and how to aim the thing, first making sure the dimmer switch was at full dim. If you turned it up, the safety gave you five minutes and then turned it down again. Otherwise you could accidentally vaporize whoever you were trying to call. You never used full power (Jefferson explained) for anything closer than an orbiting spacecraft.

He showed me how to find and call the Watchbird One satellite, using the scope. I got a computer. It gave me a news update. Spacecraft *Chili Bird* had safely departed the Belt Trading Post for Confinement Asteroid. Sunspot activity was on the increase, but no solar flares had yet formed.

I asked Jefferson, "These things do function as weapons, don't they?"

"In an emergency, yes."

"How?"

He showed me how to turn the dimmer switch to full bright. I fired at a darkish rock. I got a half-second burst of red flame, and a hole three inches deep and a quarter of an inch wide.

"Half a second isn't much of a message," I said.

So he showed me how to override the safety. "It burns out the sender, of course, and you get just enough time to yell, 'Help! Blowout!' That can be enough."

I handed it back. "Second," I said, "I'd like to go straight back to Hove City from here, and I'd like to take an escort. Officer Watson, would you care for a stroll?"

He said, "All right. See you later, Naomi, and don't worry."

She nodded jerkily, wearing the same stony expression she'd worn all this time.

We hadn't gone far when Watson said, "Operative Hamilton, we can adjust our helmet mikes so we won't disturb the others.

"I know how. Call me Gil."

"I'm Alan."

We set our radios for privacy. I said, "It finally hit me that I was missing the point. You and I aren't looking for the same killer as the rest of them. We think Naomi's not guilty, right?"

"She'd never kill a man from ambush."

"So we're looking for someone else. Sticking to Naomi's route won't give him to us. She never saw him."

He bought it. He relaxed, just a little. "She can't even tell us where he wasn't. That place where she watched the stars . . . he could have come after she left. Penzler saw his killer, didn't he? Jefferson says he did."

I'd known Naomi ten years ago; but Alan Watson knew her *now*. He believed her. Could I be wrong?

I filed the question. "Penzler says he saw something, but he can't even describe the suit. Something human, past the tilted rock. So let's walk toward the tilted rock, taking our time and looking around."

We walked through pools of glare and shadow, with

almost no in-between. The colors were mostly browns and grays and whites. Alan said, "I wish I knew what to look for. It's a shame she didn't lose something."

I shrugged that off. "We aren't looking for anything Naomi dropped. This is where the killer had to be. We check the high points because he had to have a view of Chris's window. We look for tracks of a vehicle, or burn marks from a rocket, anything that could get him out of here before the police started looking for him. He had ten minutes, or more. And look for pieces of a laser. I would have found a laser, but it could have been broken up."

"Your imaginary arm?"

Skeptical. He'd have his chance to sneer at my imaginary arm . . . when I testified for the prosecution against Naomi.

The thought of Naomi being broken up for spare parts gave me the creeps. I could never be neutral where Naomi was concerned. But say that love and hate could add to make indifference . . . say I could feel nothing for Naomi. It would *still* be like taking scissors to a George Barr painting. Vandalism.

Alan said, "That flat-topped rock where she watched the stars would have been perfect, wouldn't it?"

"Yeah. A beautiful view of Chris's window. What I don't believe is that she'd lead us there. Alan, would a lunie go sightseeing on the Moon at night?"

He laughed. "A lunie can always wait two weeks. A tourist has to go home." The grim look returned. "Most tourists pick daytime. It does look funny. Dammit."

Light and shadow. All moonscape and no clues. Every time we walked into full sunlight I had to blink against the glare. My visor took a fraction of a second to darken, and it was too long. We took the easy paths, but we stopped to climb obvious vantage points.

The silence was getting to me. I asked, "Was your father named after the city itself?"

"Oh . . . partly. *The* Jacob Hovestraydt, the man who founded the city, was my great-grandfather. And he had two daughters, and one didn't have children, and the other had Dad and my three aunts. So we're the direct genetic line. Dad was practically *born* Mayor. We've talked about it, how he grew up... Hey, stay away from there. You don't know how deep it is."

I'd been about to wade through a dust pool, scuffing my feet, looking for pieces of a laser. But he was right, of course.

I said, "I'd like another crack at the projection room. Could you get me that?"

"I think so."

"Did you ever show Naomi the projection room?"

He stopped walking. "How'd you know?"

"I just wondered."

We marched our crooked path in silence for a time. Then Alan said, "Every time some offworlder bigwig showed up he had to meet the kid. Me. Once upon a time I told Dad I didn't like it. He said he went through the same thing, when his grandfather was Mayor. And his mother picked his school courses for him. Political science, air cycle engineer-

ing, ecology, economics. His first job was in the Garden. Then he was in Maintenance, tending the air system."

"And you? Are you being groomed for Mayor?"

"Maybe. Dad was in the police, too, for awhile. I'm not sure I'll ever want to run Hovestraydt City ... and I'm sure Dad wouldn't force me, and I'm not sure I could. I don't want to now. I want to travel. Look, Gil, we've almost reached the tilted rock. That's too close."

"I wonder. In the first place, I don't trust a Belter's sense of distance on the Moon."

"Mmm ... yes. In fact ... the closer the killer was, the better the chance Penzler would see him. And Naomi wouldn't have, because she was further west. He could have been just behind the rock."

"Yeah, and we'll look."

"He'd have had to be in sunlight, wouldn't he, for Penzler to see him?" Alan squatted, then leapt. Soared. Graceful as all hell. His parabola peaked at the rock's rounded tip, and he clutched it with all four limbs, then began his own investigations.

To me it seemed a precarious perch for an aspiring marksman.

From Chris's window the tilted rock had looked like an elongated egg. But the side in darkness was almost flat. I played my headlamp over it. The surface was rough and white.

I scraped my gloved fingers over it. Crumbly white stuff adhered to my fingers. It disappeared as I watched. What the hell?

"No laser parts, no footprints, no puffer tracks, nothing," Alan said. "And there's too much dust around. If he has any brains, the killer wouldn't have been walking where there's dust. Gil, we'll have to backtrack."

"I don't think so. I don't think Chris saw his killer."

"What?"

"Why would the killer be in sunlight? He'd be half blind in the glare. It was just dawn, with most of this region in shadow. He'd have had to go *looking* for sunlight to stand in so Chris could see him. It's plain silly."

"Then what *did* he see?"

"I don't know yet. I want another look at Chris's room."

"Gil, what's your stake in this?"

"Aesthetic. She's too beautiful to be broken up." Too flippant. I tried again. "I loved her once and I hated her once. Now she's an old friend in trouble. You?"

"I love her."

We weren't looking for clues now. The tilted rock was behind us; Penzler couldn't have seen anything here. Like the keen-eyed Indian in his forest, or the street-wise mugger on his home turf, Alan Watson knew this part of the Moon. He'd see anything worth seeing. To me it was all moonscape.

I did get him talking about the Conference.

"Six out of ten of you are offworlders," he said. "We don't even have a voting majority. I can see why some citizens don't like that. But they're wrong. The Moon is a kind of halfway house between the mud and the sky . . . between Earth and the Belt. We gain some advantages from that, but we have to keep you both satisfied too. The organ bank problem doesn't make that any easier."

His lecturer's manner made him seem older, somehow. If he went into politics, he'd succeed at it.

"Might I ask, are these your father's views too?"

"We've talked about it, but I'm not just quoting him." He smiled. "The last Conference established the holding tanks. Even if Naomi's convicted, she still goes into a holding tank for six months. Six months to prove she's innocent, and I'm very glad of that."

"Wups. Alan, does she know that? She may be more scared than she has to be."

"Oh, good Lord!" He was horrified.

"So you never told her. So make an opportunity. Can she have visitors?"

"She's in her own room with the phone turned off and the door geared to reject her voice. I'm sure a policeman could visit her. I just didn't think. The trial's set for day after tomorrow, and she thinks that's it, the end. I'll tell her, Gil.

Gil, what are you doing?"

We had reached Hovestraydt City, and I was hard up against Chris Penzler's window. I said, "Checking the scene of the crime from the other side, kid."

I noted with approval that I was in the fields of three cameras. Our clumsy killer might conceivably want to plant a small bomb on the window.

I peered in. Chris was on his back on the bed, covered with foam plastic from chin to navel and armpit to armpit. The mobile autodoc was standing above him like a polished steel nursemaid.

"Alan, come here a second. Do you see anything like a miniature hologram in there? On a wall, or the table?"

"... No."

"Neither do I. Dammit."

"Why?"

"Maybe it was moved. I still can't see our half-competent marksman sticking his face into sunlight, blinding himself, just before he fired. I thought maybe Chris had a holo of his mother or someone on the wall, and he saw it reflected in the window just before he got shot. But there's nothing."

"No."

The door opened, and closed behind Harry McCavity. The doctor prodded his unconscious patient for a bit, then moved to the autodoc screen and typed, read the screen for a bit, typed again ... ran his hands through his fluffy brown hair in a swift gesture that changed nothing ... turned around, and jumped a yard in the air when he saw faces peering in the window.

I gestured in a curve to the left. *We'll come through the airlock.* He glared and gestured back. *Up Uranus!*

A few minutes later we knocked at the door and he let us in. "We were looking around," Alan said lamely.

"For what?" McCavity demanded.

I said, "A hologram portrait. My idea. Have you seen anything that might fit?"

"No."

"It's important—"

"No!"

"Can he answer questions?" I waved at Chris Penzler.

"No. Let him alone, he's doing fine. He'll be mobile tomorrow ... not comfortable, but mobile. Ask him then. Gil, are you booked for dinner?"

"No. What time do you like?"

"Say half an hour. We can check with Ms. Grimes, see if she's off duty. Perhaps she can join us."

5.

The Conference Table

We'd chosen a table in a far corner of the dining level. Lunie diners tended to cluster around the Garden. We could barely see the Garden, and nobody was in eavesdropping distance.

"It isn't just that we aren't man and wife," McCavity said, stabbing the air with splay-ended chopsticks. "We can't even keep the same hours. We enjoy each other ... don't we?"

Taffy nodded happily.

"I need constant reassurance, my dear. Gil, we enjoy each other, but when we see each other it's generally over an open patient. I'm glad for Taffy that you're here. Isn't this kind of thing supposed to be normal on Earth?"

"Well," I said, "it's normal where I've lived ... California, Kansas, Australia ... Over most of the Earth we tend to keep recreational sex separate from having children. There are the Fertility Laws, of course. The government doesn't tell people *how* to use their birthrights, but we do check the baby's tissue rejection spectrum to see *which* father has used up a birthright. Don't get the idea that Earth is all one culture. The Arabs are back to *harems*, for God's sake, and so were the Mormons, for awhile."

"Harems? What about the birthrights?"

"The harems are recreation, as far as the shiek is concerned, and of course he uses up his own birthrights. When they're gone the ladies take sperm from some healthy genius with an unlimited birthright and the right skin color, and the shiek raises the children as the next generation of aristocrats."

Harry ate while he thought. Then, "It sounds wonderful, by Allah! But for us, having children is a big thing. We tend to stay faithful. I'm the freak. And I know of a lunie who fathered a child for two good friends ... but I could maybe get killed for naming them."

I said, "Okay, we're a *menage a* at least *trois*. But you would like it noised abroad that Taffy and I are steady roommates."

"It would be convenient."

"Would it be convenient for *me*? Harry, I gather lunies

don't like that sort of thing. There are four lunie delegates in the Conference. I can't alienate them."

Taffy was frowning. "Futz! I hadn't thought of that."

Harry said, "I did. Gil, it'll *help* you. What the lunie citizen *really* wants to know is that you aren't running around compromising the honor of lunie women."

I looked at Taffy. She said, "I think he's right. I can't swear to it."

"Okay."

We ate. It was mostly vegetables, fresh, with good variety. I had almost finished a side dish, beef with onions and green pepper over rice, before I wondered. Beef?

I looked up into Harry's grin. "Imported," he said, and laughed as my jaw dropped. "No, not from Earth! Can you imagine the delta-V? Imported from Tycho. They've got an underground bubble big enough to graze cattle. It costs like blazes, of course. We're fairly wealthy here."

Dessert was strawberry shortcake, with whipped cream from Tycho. The coffee *was* imported from Earth, but freeze-dried. I wondered if they saved anything that way, given that the water in coffee beans had to be imported anyway ... then kicked myself. Lunies don't import water. They import hydrogen. They run the hydrogen past heated oxygen-bearing rock to get water vapor.

So I sipped my coffee and asked, "May we talk business?"

"None of us are squeamish," McCavity said.

"The wound, then. Would a layer of bathwater spread the beam that much?"

"I don't know. Nobody knows. It's never happened before."

"Your best guess, then."

"Gil, it had to be enough, unless you've got another explanation."

"Mmm ... there was a case in Warsaw where a killer put a dot of oil over the aperture of a laser. The beam was supposed to spread a little, just enough that the police couldn't identify the weapon. It would have worked fine if he hadn't got drunk and bragged about it."

McCavity shrugged his eyebrows. "Not here. Any damn fool would *guess* it was a message laser."

"We know the beam spread. We're speculating."

Harry's eyes went distant and dreamy. "Would the oil vaporize?"

"Sure. Instantly."

"The beam would constrict in mid-burn. That would fit. The hole in Penzler's chest looked like the beam changed width in the middle of the burn."

"It constricted?"

"It constricted, or expanded, or there's something we haven't thought of."

"Futz. Okay. Do you know Naomi Mitchison?"

"Vaguely." Harry seemed to withdraw a little.

"Not intimately?"

"No."

Taffy was looking at him. We waited.

"I grew up here," Harry said abruptly. "I *never* make proposals to a woman unless I have reason to think they'll be accepted. Okay, I must have read the signals wrong. She reacted like an insulted married lunie woman! So I apologised and went away, and we haven't spoken since. You're right, flatlanders aren't all the same. A week ago I would have said we were friends. Now ... no, I don't know the lady."

"Do you hate her?"

"What? No."

Taffy said, "Maybe your killer doesn't care if Penzler lives or dies. Maybe it's Naomi he wants to hurt."

I mulled that. "I don't like it. First, how would he know he could make it stick? There *might* have been someone else out there. Second, it gives us a whole damn *city* full of suspects." I noticed, or imagined, Harry's uneasiness. "Not you, Harry. You sweated blood to save Chris. It would have been trivial to kill him while the 'doc was cutting him up."

Harry grinned. "So what? It was already an organ bank crime for Naomi."

"Yes, but he saw something. He might remember more."

Taffy asked, "Who else wouldn't want to frame Naomi?"

"I'm really not taking the idea too seriously," I said, "but ... I guess I'd want to know who she insulted. Who made passes and got slapped down, and who took it badly."

Harry said, "You won't find many lunie suspects."

"The men are too careful?"

"That, and— No offense, my dear, but Naomi isn't beautiful by lunie standards. She's stocky."

"What," wondered Taffy, "does that make me?"

Harry grinned at her. "Stocky. I told you I was a freak."

She grinned back at that tall, narrow offshoot of human stock ... and I found myself grinning too. They did get along. It was a pleasure to watch them.

We broke it up soon afterward. Taffy was on duty, and I needed my sleep.

The City Hall complex was four stories deep, with the Mayor's office on the ground level. A room on the second level was reserved for the Conference.

I got there at 0800. Eight-foot-tall Bertha Carmody was in animated discussion with a small, birdlike Belt woman in late middle age. They broke off long enough to introduce the stranger: Hildegarde Quifting, Fourth Speaker for the Belt Government.

Chris Penzler was in a bulky armchair equipped with safety straps and a ground-effect skirt. Soft foam covered his chest. He seemed to be brooding on his wrongs.

I said hello anyway. He looked up. "You'll find coffee and rolls on the side table," he said, and tried to wave in the right direction. "Ow!"

"Hurts?"

"Yah."

I got coffee in a small-mouthed bottle with a foam plastic sleeve. Other delegates trickled in until we were all present.

A lunie I hadn't met, Charles Ward of Copernicus, moved to elect a chairman, then nominated Bertha Carmody of Tycho Dome. With four lunies out of ten delegates, the chairman was bound to be a lunie, so I voted for Bertha. So did everybody else. The lunies seemed surprised at their easy victory. But Bertha was a good choice; she had the loudest voice among us.

We spent the morning covering old ground.

Belt and Moon and United Nations had each their own axes to grind. Officially the Moon was a satellite of Earth and was subject to the United Nations law, in which even minor crimes carried the death penalty: laws designed not only to punish the guilty, but also to supply transplant organs to the innocent voting public.

The ethical gap between Earth and Belt was as vast as the physical gap. On Earth the hospitals had been supplied by criminals for well over a hundred years. When Luke Garner was young the death penalty had been revived for murder, kidnapping, treason and the like. As medical techniques improved and spread to the have-not nations, demands on the public organ banks had grown. The death penalty was imposed for armed robbery, rape, burglary. A plea of insanity became worthless. Eventually felons died for income tax evasion or driving while high on funny chemicals.

Belt hospitals kept organ banks, but there were major differences. The Belt used fewer transplants. Belters tend to let evolution take care of the careless ones; they are not egalitarians. Space accidents don't tend to leave medical cases anyway. The Belt didn't perform its own executions. Up to twenty years ago their practice had been to ship convicts to Earth, and buy the organs back. In theory their law would not be affected by the flatlanders' greed for life.

The Moon's shallower gravity well made it a far better choice as the Belt's place of execution.

So the first Conference was called, and strange were the results.

There had been major compromises at the Conference of 2105. The biggest was the holding tanks. They were unique throughout the solar system. The Belt had insisted that they be built, and the UN had capitulated. The holding tanks would hold a convict inactivated, but alive and healthy, for six months. If new evidence was found, the convict could be revived.

Twenty years later, that solution was under fire.

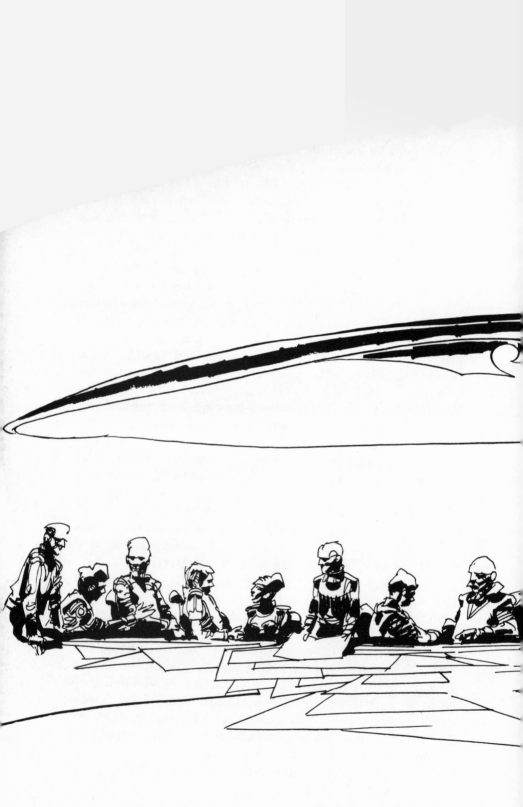

Hildegarde Quifting wanted a rundown on the past twenty years of lunar jurisprudence. In particular, had the holding tanks ever been forced to disgorge a living felon?

Charles Ward obliged. He was six eleven or so, in his late thirties, a frail dark man with a receding hairline. In a colorless voice he told us that over the past twenty years some six thousand felons had passed through the lunar courts and hospitals. Just under a thousand were lunies. The Belt felons had been convicted by Belt courts; lunar hospitals served only as execution grounds. No conviction had yet been reversed.

Ward represented Copernicus Dome, actually a complex of domes plus a metals mine, the site of one of the Moon's three major hospital complexes. Ward had come armed with graphs and maps and statistics. Average of a hundred and twenty executions a year, mostly Belters shipped in via the Belt Trading Post and the mass driver in Grimalde crater. The hospital took nearly four hundred patients a year, mostly lunies, the numbers rising over the years as the lunar population increased. I listened carefully. Copernicus was where Naomi would be sent if she was convicted.

Lunch was delivered around noon. We talked in low voices while we ate, until Carmody called us to order. At once Marion Shaeffer demanded to know whether the lunar hospitals shipped as much transplant material out as came to them through the Belt courts.

Ward answered, a bit superciliously, that Belt transplants tended to be not quite the right shape; that bones and muscles from Belter arms and legs, for instance, would be drastically too short for a lunie. This seemed obvious enough, but it wasn't what Marion meant. She wanted to know how much transplant material the Moon shipped to Earth.

Quite a lot.

The Conference was polarizing. Belters and flatlanders were opposite poles, with the lunies in the middle. To frail old Hildegarde Quifting, our approach to the organ bank problem was monstrous: death penalties imposed at every opportunity to keep the voting citizens alive and healthy. To Jabez Stone of the General Assembly, a criminal was lucky

to redeem himself in *any* way, and Belters need not act so damn superior. When a man orders a steak, a steer must be mutilated, then murdered. How many transplants were keeping Quifting alive?

Carmody ruled that out of order. Quifting insisted on answering it anyway. She had *never* had a transplant, she said belligerently. I noticed uncomfortable expressions among the delegates. Maybe they noticed mine.

It was a long session. The break for dinner came none too soon.

I fell in beside Chris Penzler's softly whispering air-cushion chair. "You didn't say much. Are you up to this?"

"Oh, I'm up to it." He smiled a passable smile, that faded. "I feel mortal," he said. "Having a hole shot through him can make a man think. I could *die*. I have one daughter. I never had time for more, I was too busy making money, making a career, and then ... there was a solar flare while I was en route to Mercury, and now I'm sterile. When I die, she'll be all that's left of me. Almost."

I said, "The quality of their lives is as important as their number."

Trite, but he nodded thoughtfully. Then, "Somebody hates me enough to kill me."

"Does Naomi Mitchison hate you that much?"

He scowled. "She has no reason. Oh, she's strange enough, and she doesn't like me, but ... I wish I knew. I hope to God it's her."

Of course. If it wasn't Naomi, then the clumsy killer was still loose.

I asked, "Do you keep holograms in your room? Or statues of any kind?"

He stared. "No."

"Futz. Is your phone working all right?"

"Yah, it's working well. Why?"

"Just a thought. Now, you said you were looking past a big tilted rock when you saw somebody. Which side of the rock?"

"I don't remember." He considered. "That's very strange.

I *don't* remember. *Mayor Hove?*" he bellowed.

Hove was just coming up a spiral stairwell at the end of the hall. He turned, startled. "Hello, Chris, Gil. How's the Conference going?"

I said, "There's a certain amount of friction—"

Chris interrupted. "Can you let us into your office?"

"Of course. Why?"

"I want to look out the window." He seemed feverishly excited.

The Mayor shrugged. He led the way upstairs.

His office was big, roomy. The computer terminal built into the desk hooked into the hologram wall and into two more screens. There was a foot and a half of keyboard with a roll-top cover. A hologram wall looked out on Jovian storms, seen from closer than Amalthea, swirling like a million shades of paint poured into a whirlpool. Endless storms big enough to swallow the Earth. Hovestraydt Watson must have a big ego, I thought. How else could he live and work next to *that*?

The picture window looked south into a blazing moonscape. Chris edged as close as he could to the window. "I can't see it. We'll have to go to my room."

"What's it all about?" the Mayor asked.

"I was looking past a large boulder just before the beam burned me. I must have seen the killer to one side or the other, but I can't—"

"Are you sure he wasn't closer than the rock?"

Penzler screwed his eyes shut. After a moment he said, "Almost. He'd have to be a midget to show that small, that close. I wish I could be sure."

I said, "Chris, I thought maybe you saw a reflection from a small hologram in your room, or maybe from the phone screen. Is that possible?"

Chris shrugged. Mayor Hove said, "The phone would have to be on, wouldn't it? It would have been facing Chris, if it was working right. Chris, did you call anyone while you were in the tub?"

"No. And my phone system is working."

So we went down the hall to Chris's room, all three of us.

Chris pointed out the tilted rock Alan Watson and I had investigated. We studied it for a good minute before he said, "I simply cannot remember. But he was almost twice as far as the rock."

I called from my room. "I want to talk to Naomi Mitchison," I told the desk sergeant, "preferably in person."
He looked at me. "You're not her lawyer."
"I didn't claim to be."

He took his time thinking it over. "I'll put you through to her lawyer." He rang, waited, then said, "Mr. Boone isn't there. His answering bug says he's in conference with a client."

"So let me talk to them both."

He went into a brown study. I said, "Then put me through to Sergeant Drury, if *that's* possible."

His relief showed. He made the call. The phone screen went blank, and Laura Drury's voice said, "Just a minute. Gil Hamilton, isn't it?"

"Yes. I'm trying to get permission to talk to Ms. Mitchison. The desk sergeant is giving me static."

"Let's see, her lawyer is supposed to be with her. I'll call him on her phone. He's a public defender, Artemus Boone."

"Lunie?"

"Yes. Did you learn anything from going over her course?"

"Nothing conclusive."

The screen lighted. Laura Drury was just completing the act of zipping up a pale gold jump suit. I gathered the picture had caught her a split second too soon. The zipper had hesitated at her bosom; and well it might. She looked flustered; she tugged hard; the zipper went up. I repressed a smile.

"Jefferson thinks she was lying," she said, "but he can't tell what she was lying about."

I thought so too. "I'd like to know more about that trek myself," I said. "I have to go through this Boone, is that right? If you can't convince him, may I talk to him myself? I'd like to help her."

"I'll find out. Stand by." She put me on hold.

She called back a minute later. "They won't see you. They won't talk to you either. I'm sorry."

"Futz! Is that just her lawyer's word?"

"I think he talked to her first, off camera."

"Thanks, Laura." I called the phone off. I debated schemes for getting through to her anyway, and gave up on them. I didn't really have a lot to say to Naomi.

6.

The Lunar Law

The Committee met again at 0800. I'd had breakfast with Taffy, but the rest of us were sipping and munching when Bertha Carmody called us to order.

Charles Ward asked for the floor. "It strikes me that our differences are all concerned with matters of the lunar law and the manner in which it is enforced. Is this the case?"

He got noises signifying agreement. "Then let me remind you all," said that frail dark beanpole, "that the trial of Naomi Mitchison for the attempted murder of Chris Penzler begins in one hour. Some of us are likely to be called as witnesses. Mr. Penzler, in particular, is still recovering from his wounds. His mind is likely to be on the trial."

Chris nodded, and winced in pain. "You may be right. I wouldn't be concentrating."

Ward spread his hands wide. "Then in the interests of actually observing lunar justice in action, why don't we all adjourn to the courtroom?"

We voted eight to two in favor. We adjourned to the courtroom.

The courtroom was a place of beauty. Its design was standard: high podium for the judge, rails separating the spectators from the accused and the jury. It was the thousand-year-old English courtroom design, originally intended to protect the accused from the victim's family. But one whole wall was glass, and it overlooked the Garden.

Mirrors caught the raw lunar sunlight and diffused it down upon dozens of ledges of plants, down along the great redwood to its long, tangled roots. The air was full of wings. No plant grew that didn't have a use; but the prettiest plants, artichokes and apple trees and so forth, were the most accessible; and the dancing fountains weren't only for irrigation, and the winding paths weren't only for the farmers. The Garden was designed for pleasure.

I thought how terrible it must be to look out on the Garden and wait to be condemned to death.

Naomi was watching the Garden. Her golden hair was piled high in a coiled arrangement that must represent hours of work. She had taken particular care with dress and cosmetics. The butterfly tattoo was gone. She seemed composed, with terror hiding underneath. When her lunie lawyer whispered to her, her answers were curt. She must know that if she started screaming they would fill her full of tranquilizers.

Was she guilty? My judgment could never be impartial where Naomi was concerned.

Chris Penzler thought she was. He watched Naomi's eyes while he gave his testimony. "I was taking a bath. I stood up and reached for a towel. I thought I saw something outside the window, a man or a woman. Then there was a flare of red light. It struck me in the chest, threw me back in the water and knocked me unconscious."

The prosecuting lawyer was a pale blond woman over seven feet tall, massing no more than I do. She had an elvish triangular face, quite lovely, quite perfect, and quite without human weakness. She asked, "What color was the suit? Did it have markings on it?"

Penzler shook his head. "I didn't have time to see."

"But you saw only one person."

"Yes," he said, and looked at Naomi.

She probed. "Was it a local? We tend to be taller and thinner."

Chris didn't laugh, though others did. "I don't know. It was less than a second, then ... it was like being run through with a red hot jousting lance."

"How far away?"

"Three to four hundred meters. I can't judge distances here."

"Would Naomi Mitchison have any reason to hate you?"

"I've wondered about that." Chris hesitated, then said, "Four years ago, Mrs. Mitchison applied for emigration to the Belt. Her application was turned down." Again he hesitated. "By me."

Naomi's surprise and anger were obvious.

Prosecution asked, "Why?"

"I knew her. She wasn't qualified. The Belt environment

kills careless people. She would have been a danger to herself and everyone around her." Chris Penzler's ears and neck were quite pink.

Prosecution was through with him. Naomi's lawyer cross-examined him briefly. "You say you knew Mrs. Mitchison. How well?"

"I knew Naomi and Itch Mitchison briefly, five years ago, when I was on Earth. We attended a few parties together. Itch wanted to know about buying mining stocks, and I got him some details."

Naomi was moving her lips without sound. I read the words on her lips: *Liar, liar.*

"You believe you saw your assassin out on the Moon. Could you be mistaken, or could you have missed others out there?"

Chris laughed. "I saw a human shape blazing against the dark. It was *night on the Moon!* There could have been an army hidden in the shadows. For that matter, perhaps I only saw a pattern of reflections. I only saw it for a split second, then *bang.*"

Prosecution dismissed Chris and called a lunie cop I didn't know. He testified that there was indeed a message laser missing from the weapons room. Defense tried to get him to say that the door would open only to the police. What the cop said was that the lock responded to voice and retinae prints, and that it was governed by the Hovestraydt City computer, the same that operated every door and safe lock in the city, not to mention the water and air.

Prosecution then asked that Naomi's records, beamed from Earth, be read into the record. I remembered: Naomi had been a computer programmer.

The elf woman turned with floating grace in lunar gravity. "Call Gilbert Hamilton."

I was aware that I moved to the witness chair with a flatlander's clumsiness, treading air and half-falling at every step.

"Your name and occupation?"

"Gilbert Gilgamesh Hamilton. I'm an ARM."

"Are you here on the Moon in that capacity?"

"It's not my regular beat," I said, and got suppressed laughter. "I'm here for the Conference to Review Lunar Law."

She didn't need to go into that. The judge and three jurors were all lunies; they'd have been following the Conference via the boob cube. She led me through the details of Tuesday night: the midnight call, the scene in Penzler's room, the trek to the projection room.

Then she asked, "Are you sometimes called Gil the Arm?"

"Yes."

"Why?"

"I've got an imaginary arm." I had to smile at the baffled looks. "It's a combination of psychic powers. During the years I spent asteroid mining, I lost my right arm. I got it replaced eventually—"

"In what fashion?"

"It's a transplant. No telling who it belonged to. It came out of the stock in trade of a captured organlegger."

"Please continue."

"With just the stump left, I found I was using a kind of ghost arm. It works best in low gravity. I've got two of the recognised psychic powers, esper and telekinesis, but they're restricted by my imagination. I can't reach further than the stretch of a real arm."

"Returning to the projection room," she said. "Did you search the landscape in an attempt to find any suspect who might have been overlooked?"

"For a suspect or for a discarded weapon, yes."

"In what fashion did you search?"

"I ran my imaginary fingers through the projected moonscape." There was a whisper of giggling from the audience. I'd expected that. "I sifted shadows, dust pools, anything big enough to hide a message laser."

"Or a human being? Would you have found a human being, or were you, let us say, tuned only to the shape and feel of a message laser?"

"I'd have found a human being."

She turned me over to defense.

Artemus Boone stood seven feet plus, with craggy features, a full black beard, and thick black hair. To me he looked like a wandering ghoul, but I was biased. The lunie jurors might be seeing an elongated Abe Lincoln.

"You came for the Conference to Review Lunar Law. When did it begin?"

"Yesterday."

"Have you revised many of our laws yet?" He'd decided I was an adverse witness.

"We haven't had time to revise anything," I said.

"Not even regarding the holding tanks?"

Hey, weren't our doings supposed to be secret? But nobody objected. I said, "That one may never be settled."

"How were you chosen to represent the United Nations viewpoint, Mr. Hamilton?"

"I was a Belt miner for seven years. Now I'm an ARM. It gives me two of the three crucial viewpoints. I'm picking up the lunie viewpoint as best I can."

"As best you can," Boone said dubiously. "Well, then. The pleasantly convenient manner in which Naomi Mitchison has supplied us with exactly one suspect may have led us to overlook something. You were present when she was brought in. Was she carrying a weapon?"

"No."

"You say you searched for a message laser. Just how much imaginary moonscape did you run your imaginary fingers through?"

"I searched the badlands west of the city, the area Chris Penzler could have seen from his bathtub. I searched as far as the western peaks, and some of the far slopes."

"You found no weapon?"

"None."

"Psychic powers have always been undependable, haven't they? Science was reluctant even to recognize their existence, and the law was slow in allowing psychics to testify. Tell me, Mr. Hamilton: if your unusual talent missed finding a message laser, could you not have overlooked a man?"

"It's possible, certainly."

Defense was through with me. The cold-eyed elf woman asked me, "What if the gun had been broken up and the pieces discarded? Would you have found it?"

"I don't know."

They let me go and I sat down.

Prosecution called an expert witness, an oriental-seeming man who turned out to be a lunie cop. He was actually shorter than I am. He testified that he had examined Naomi's pressure suit and found it to be working satisfactorily. In the course of tests he had worn the suit outside. "It was a tight fit," he said.

"Did you notice anything else?"

"I noticed the smell. The suit is some years old, and the molecular filter badly needs cleaning. After some hours of wear certain fatigue poisons build up in the recycled air, and it begins to smell."

They called Octavia Budrys, and I started to catch on.

"The police handed me a pressure suit," she said, "and told me to gear up. I did. I suppose they chose me because I'm not used to space. I barely know how to put on a pressure suit."

"Did you notice anything?"

"Yes, there was a faint chemical smell, not so much unpleasant as, well, ominous. I would have had it repaired before I tried to wear it outside."

The killer fired as soon as Chris Penzler stood up in his tub. He'd already waited a good long while. Why not wait a moment longer while Penzler got out?

Because the smell in Naomi Mitchison's suit made her think her air supply was going bad. She was afraid to wait.

I wasn't convinced. Any given killer might have lost patience, waiting in lunar discomfort while Chris wallowed in his tub. But it was a point against Naomi.

The court broke for lunch. After lunch the defense called Naomi Mitchison.

Boone kept it short. He asked Naomi if she had stolen a message laser and tried to kill Chris Penzler with it. She swore she hadn't. He asked her what she was doing during the period in question. She told the court more or less what she'd told us, adding details. She swore that she had never had any reason to dislike Chris Penzler until now.

Boone mentioned that he might have further questions, and turned her over to the prosecution.

The elf woman did not waste our time.

"On September 6, 2121, did you apply for emigration to the asteroid belt society?"

"I did."

"Why?"

"Things had gone all wrong," Naomi said. "I wanted out."

"How did they go wrong?"

"My husband tried to kill me. I got to one of the bathrooms, locked the door and went out the window. He killed our little girl and then himself. That was in June."

"Why did he do it?"

"I don't know. I've thought about it. I don't know."

"Let me see if I can help," the elf woman said. "The records show that Itch Mitchison was a professional comedian. The basis of his humor was an image that used to be called *macho:* a man who expects sexual exclusivity from his woman, and who expects of himself unlimited potency and attractiveness to women. Was that the case?"

"More or less."

"What was he like in his private life?"

"Pretty much the same. Some of that was a put-on, but . . . I think that's the way he was."

"You had a little girl?"

"Miranda. Born January 4, 2117. She was four and a half years old when Itch killed her." Her calm had cracked.

"Had you and your husband applied for a second child?"

"Yes. But by then Itch's grandmother was in the organ banks. She . . . is this necessary?"

"No. It will be read into the record."

"Just say she went crazy, then. The Fertility Board decided it was congenital. They had his record of asthma trouble, childhood diseases. . . The upshot was that I could have children, but Itch couldn't, and he bloody well didn't want me to. We talked about my using artificial insemination. He got terribly angry. That old *macho* image wasn't just about seduction, did you know that?" Brittle laughter. "When you sire a *lot* of babies, then you're *macho.*"

"Was your love life affected by these developments?"

"It was killed dead. And he did have that congenital tendency. Eventually he . . . he snapped."

"Three months later you applied to the Belt."

"Yes."

"And Chris Penzler blocked you."

"I didn't know that. I never had reason to hate Chris Penzler," she said. "I didn't know why my application was turned down. But that vindictive bastard had reason to hate me! He made a pass at me once, and I slapped him down good!"

"Physically? Did you actually strike him?"

"No, of course not. I told him to go to hell. I told him that if he ever came near me again I'd tell Itch. Itch would have knocked him silly. That's *macho* too."

I guessed she'd made a point in her favor. Lunies wouldn't be familiar with open marriages.

The elf woman thought differently. "Very well, Mr. Penzler made indecent proposals to you, a married woman. Surely that might be reason for you to hate and despise him? Especially after what later happened to your marriage."

Naomi shook her head. "He didn't cause that."

The prosecution dismissed her and called Alan Watson.

Of the team that had tried to follow Naomi's ill-timed attempt to play tourist, four were called as witnesses. They did Naomi little good. Naomi had led them straight to the scene of the crime. Her knowledge of the terrain was spotty at best. The best reason for believing her was that she would have had to be crazy to lie.

I ate dinner alone and went back to my room. It was my mind that was exhausted; I'd had no exercise, yet I felt like sleeping for a week. But I checked my phone before I dropped off.

I had messages from Taffy and from Desiree Porter.

Taffy and Harry were both free Friday. They planned to explore the shops of the Belt Trading Post. Would I like to join them? Feel free to add a friend, female preferred. I phoned back, but Taffy wasn't in and neither was Harry. I left a message: sorry, I was tied up in the Conference and a

murder trial.

I tried to call Naomi's room. Her phone refused my call. I wasn't up to fighting with Artemus Boone.

And I didn't want to talk to a newstaper. I called off the lights and flopped back. And the phone said, "Phone call, Mr. Hamilton. Pho—"

"Chiron, answer phone."

Tom Reinecke was standing behind the seated Desiree, their faces level. It was a nice effect, and they knew it. I said, "What do you two want?"

"News," said Desiree. "Are you getting anywhere with the Conference?"

"Secret. Anyway, we postponed it."

"We heard that. Do you think Naomi Mitchison will be convicted?"

"Up to the jury."

"You're a big help—"

Tom cut in smoothly. "It's the speed of the trial that impressed us. Why do you suppose it went so fast?"

"Oh, hell." I was fully awake. "They think they've got a locked room murder. One suspect, locked out on the Moon. If they could eliminate Naomi they'd invent themselves a real problem. *No* suspects. So they aren't really trying."

"How would you go about it?" Tom asked, while Desiree was saying, "Would you change the law?"

They'd caught me half asleep and got me talking. It served me right. "Changing the law wouldn't make anything different. How would I get her off? I'd prove she wasn't there, or I'd prove someone else was, or maybe I'd prove the killer wasn't where we thought he was."

Tom asked, "How would you do that?"

"I'm tired. Go away and leave me alone."

Desiree asked, "Is she guilty?"

"Chiron, phone off. No calls for eight hours."

I didn't know.

Getting to sleep took a long time.

7.

Last Night and Morning After

We discussed the trial over our rolls and coffee next morning. Belters and flatlanders both expressed surprise at its speed and at the number of jurors.

The lunies took affront. They asserted that the accused's agony of anticipation should be as brief as possible. As for the jury, the Moon had never had a large population with vast leisure. Three were enough. A larger jury would only get tangled in a dozen different viewpoints, like any committee. Like our own.

It got rather heated.

Chris Penzler was out of his travel chair, but foam bandaging still bulked out his shirt, and he moved like an old man. He wasn't inclined to join the discussions. Neither was I. Once I tried to suggest that the length of a trial should depend on the complexity of the case. Nobody much liked that, and in fact Marion Shaeffer insisted that I was biased in the accused's favor. I dropped it.

Presently Bertha Carmody called us to order, said a few words intended to soothe ruffled feelings, and adjourned us to the courtroom.

I wasn't called again. Chris Penzler was. He testified at length as to his relationship to Itch and Naomi on Earth.

He said he had seen Naomi when she arrived at Hovestraydt City. She had given him a cold glare, and he had returned it, and they had avoided each other since. He repeated that he couldn't describe what he saw before he was shot. Lunie, Belter, flatlander: he couldn't say.

He didn't seem to be trying to hurt Naomi. It was as if he was trying to work out a puzzle, with the court's help.

Defense called Dr. Harry McCavity, who testified that from the nature of the wound the beam must have spread abnormally. Asked to agree that something other than a message laser had been used—something cobbled together by an amateur, for instance, so that it didn't collimate very

well—McCavity dithered. The hole in Penzler was not *that* much too big. And, damn him, he raised my suggestion of a drop of oil on the aperture.

They wrapped it up faster than I would have believed.

At eleven hundred the elf woman started her summing-up. She pointed out that Naomi had motive, method, and opportunity.

Jurisprudence did not require that motive be proved (I had wondered if that was true in lunar law), but Naomi had motive enough. Circumstances had struck Naomi a terrible blow; she had made a half-mad attempt to escape an intolerable environment; Chris Penzler had blocked it for his own motives. Prosecution made no excuse for Penzler, but his vindictive act had been the straw that broke her mind.

Method? Naomi had been a top computer programmer. Breaking the code of the Hovestraydt City computer wouldn't be easy, but her needs were not great. She needed only to enter a computer-guarded gun room without leaving a record in the computer memory.

Opportunity? Someone had fired at Penzler from the badlands west of Hovestraydt City. Penzler had seen her; a known psychic had testified that nobody else was in the vicinity. Had Naomi Mitchison fired that beam? Who else?

During his own summing-up, Boone made a big thing of the missing weapon. The jury must disregard Gil "the Arm's" testimony as to the absence of other suspects, or accept that there was no weapon either, and thus no murder. The nature of the wound indicated that the weapon was homemade, using skills Naomi Mitchison didn't have. Gil Hamilton's talent had missed it, and the killer too.

Prosecution's counterargument was concise. There had been a laser. Ignore the nature of both weapon and would-be-killer; if Hamilton couldn't find it, the weapon must have been broken up. There were dust pools to hide the parts. Jury must disregard the absence of the laser, and consider the presence of a suspect caught out on the Moon with an air system going sour.

By shortly after noon the judge was instructing the jury. By thirteen hundred the jury had retired.

We straggled off to lunch. I wasn't hungry, of course, but I managed to get Bertha Carmody talking around her sandwich.

"I wonder if they've really got enough information to make a decision," I ventured. "The summing-up seemed so ... quick."

"They've got everything they need," Bertha said. "They've got a computer with access to all the records of the trial, dossiers for everyone who was so much as mentioned, and anything in the city library. If a point of law comes up they can call the judge day or night until they bring in a verdict. What more do they need?"

They needed to have been in love with Naomi Mitchison.

I couldn't concentrate during the afternoon session. I was trying to outguess a jury several floors away. Talk flowed past me ...

"I wonder if you're not a bit quick to convict," Octavia Budrys said, "knowing that a conviction can be reversed."

"You've watched a trial," Bertha Carmody said. "Did you have any quarrel with the proceedings?"

"Only that it was so quick. I'll admit that the case seems open-and-shut. What will happen to her now?"

The delegate from Clavius said, "We've been through that. She'll spend six months in the holding tank. It's the same technology used on the slowboats, the interstellar starships, and it's quite safe. Then, barring a reversal, she'll be broken up."

"She won't be touched until then?"

"Barring an emergency, no."

"What does the lunar law call an emergency?"

That was the question that snapped me wide awake.

Ward gave us details. There *had* been emergencies. Six years ago a quake had ripped one of the domes open at Copernicus. The doctors had used everything they could get their hands on, including holding tanks. They'd preserved the felons' central nervous systems until their grace time was up. They'd done the same after the Blowout of eighteen years ago. Two years ago, there was a patient whose odd tissue rejection patterns matched a holding tank felon's...

Rare and unlikely events. Yeah. Maybe we didn't really have six months.

There were calls waiting on my phone from Sergeant Laura Drury and Artemus Boone. I took Drury's call first.

She was sitting crosslegged on a bed, quite naked. I hadn't thought lunies were that casual. Naked, she was sheer delight: brown hair three feet long floating in the room's air currents, a long, slender, graceful body with lines of hard muscle, heavy breasts that floated too, and legs that went on forever. But her words drove all prurient thoughts out of my mind.

"Gil, forgive the voice-only. I called to tell you the jury's come back," she said. "I thought you should hear it from someone you know. It's a conviction. She'll be flown to Copernicus tomorrow morning. I'm sorry."

There was no shock. I'd been expecting it.

The phone asked, "Will there be a reply?"

"Chiron, record reply. Thanks for calling, Laura, I appreciate it. Chiron, phone off."

I stared out the window for a minute before I remembered the other call.

The black-bearded lawyer was seated behind an ancient computer terminal in an equally ancient, windowless office. His message was short. "My client has asked me to ask you to call her. Her number is two-seven-one-one. You may have to get it through the police. I apologise for refusing your calls earlier, but in my judgment it was best."

Her timing was silly. The trial was over. Oh, well—

"Chiron, phone, call two-seven-one-one."

"Please identify yourself."

"Gilbert Hamilton."

I waited while the city computer compared voice prints, while it called Naomi's room, while Naomi—"Gil! Hello!"

She looked awful. She looked like a once lovely woman coming out of a year on the wire. Her gaiety was a brittle mask. I said, "Hello. Isn't your timing a little off? I might have been able to do something."

She brushed it off. "Gil, will you spend my last night with me? We used to be good friends, and I don't want to be alone."

I would have preferred a night on the rack. "There's Alan Watson. There's your lawyer."

"I've seen enough of Artemus Boone to last—Gil, he's all tied up in my mind with the trial. Please?" She hadn't even mentioned Alan.

"I'll call you back," I said.

A last night with Naomi. The thought terrified me.

Taffy wasn't answering her phone. I tried Harry McCavity's room, and got Harry.

"She's in a brush-up class on trace element dietary deficiencies," he said. "I took it last year. Flatlanders don't need it except in places like Brazil. What's up?"

"Naomi Mitchison's been convicted."

"Is she guilty?"

"For all I know. She's been lying about *something*. She wants me to spend her last night with her."

"Well? You're old friends, aren't you?"

"How would Taffy feel about that?"

He looked puzzled. "You know her. She doesn't think she owns either of us. Anyway, it's a mission of mercy. You're sitting up with a sick friend. There isn't anyone sicker than Naomi Mitchison right now." When he got no response, he asked, "What do you want to hear?"

"I want someone to talk me out of it."

He thought it over. Then, "Taffy wouldn't try. But she'll want to hold your hand when it's over, I think. I'll tell her. Maybe she can get some time early tomorrow. Shall I let you know?"

"Futz!"

"Witness is unresponsive. Does it help if I tell you I sympathize? I'll get drunk with you if she's not free."

"I may need that. Chiron, phone off. Chiron, phone, call two-seven-one-one." Futz. I was going to have to go through with it.

I found a cop outside her door. He took my retinae prints and checked them with the city computer. He grinned down at me and started to say something, looked again and changed his mind. He said instead, "You look like they're about to break *you* up."

"It feels like they already did."

He let me past.

It was party time. Naomi wore floating luminous transparencies, blue with flashes of scarlet. The butterfly fluttering on her eyelids had iridescent blue wings. She smiled and ushered me in, and for a moment I forgot why I was here. Then her eyes flicked to the clock, and mine followed. 1810, city time.

0628, city time. Early morning. Two orange hemispheres

looked me in the eye as I emerged. I looked up. The cop guarding Naomi's door had been replaced by Laura Drury.

I asked, "How long has she got?"

"Half an hour."

Futz, I already knew that. The landscape within my skull was blanketed in fog. Later I remembered the chill in Drury's voice. I was in no shape to notice then.

I said, "I hate to let her sleep and I hate to wake her up. What do I do?"

"I don't know her. If she went to sleep happy, let her sleep."

"Happy?" I shook my head. She hadn't been happy. Should I wake her? No. I said, "I want to thank you for calling. It was kind."

"That's all right."

I considered telling Laura that she'd better get her phone fixed or stop mumbling the commands. I was almost that woozy. Tell a lunie she'd exposed her nakedness to a flat-lander? Not me. I waved and turned away and staggered to the elevators.

At the ground floor level I decided I wanted to be alone. I aimed myself toward my room. I changed my mind before I got there.

Taffy studied me for a moment. Then she pulled me in, worked my rumpled clothes off, got me face down on the bed, poured oil on me and started a massage. When she felt some of the tension leaving me, she spoke. "Do you want to talk about it?"

"Um. I don't think so."

"What do you want? Coffee? Sleep?"

"More massage," I said. "She was the perfect hostess."

"It was her last chance."

"It was reminiscence time. She wanted to cover a ten year gap in one night. We did a lot of talking."

She said nothing.

"Taffy? Do you want to have children?"

Her hands stopped, then resumed kneading my calf muscle and Achilles tendon. "Some day."

"With me?"

"What brought this on?"

"Naomi. Chris Penzler. They both waited too long. I wouldn't want to wait too long."

She said, "Pregnant women don't make good surgeons. They turn clumsy. I'd have to drop my career for six or seven months. I'd want to think about that."

"Right."

"And I'd want to finish my tour here."

"Right."

"I'd want to get married. A fifteen year contract. I wouldn't want to raise a child alone."

In my fatigue-doped state I hadn't thought that far. Fifteen years! Still— "Sounds reasonable. How many birthrights do you have?"

"Just the two."

"Good. Me too. Why don't we use them both? More efficient."

She kissed the small of my back, then went back to working the bones and joints of my feet. She asked, "What did she say that got you so worked up about children?"

I tried to remember . . .

Naomi fluttered around the bar in a cloud of blue and scarlet transparencies. She made Navy grogs in huge balloon glasses with constricted rims. I gathered we weren't expected to stay sober. She asked, "What have you been doing for ten years?"

I told her how I had fled Earth for the Belt, emphasizing her part in it. I thought she'd like that. I told her how we'd set a bomb to move a small asteroid, how the asteroid had shattered and a rock splinter had driven through the ship's hull, through my right arm, through Cubes Forsythe. "I usually just say a meteor got me. But it was our own meteor."

She wanted me to show her my imaginary arm. In lunar gravity it was possible to heft the weight of the glass, now

that it was nearly empty.

She told me about life with Itch. He was savagely jealous, and an inconsiderate lover, and he slept with women who looked like genetic failures next to Naomi herself. He had the fragile ego of any half-successful comic—

"So why did you marry him?"

She shrugged.

I spoke before I thought. "Did you like him being jealous?

Maybe it kept other men at just the right distance."

"I didn't like being slapped around for it!" I was looking for a change of subject when she added, "When I was climbing out of that bathroom window I swore I'd never let a man father a child on me again. That was even before I knew Miranda was dead."

"It's a big thing to give up."

For an instant her look was wary, secretive. Then, "Maybe I'm a loser in the evolution game. You don't have children yourself, do you?"

"Not yet."

"Are you out of the evolution game?"

"Not yet." I hefted my empty glass in my imaginary hand. "Every so often someone almost kills me. Maybe ... maybe it's time."

Naomi got up so energetically that for a moment she floated. "Futz this. Let's see what's for dinner."

"There were subjects she shied away from," I told Taffy.

She was working on my shoulders. "That's not surprising."

"Granted. The organ banks, Penzler getting shot at ... and children. She chopped that off fast, and that's not surprising either, I guess."

"Gil, you didn't *grill* her, did you?"

"No!" But I'd flinched. Guilt? "I only noticed things. I think she lied on the stand. I know she did. But why?"

"She'd have had to be crazy."

"Yeah. I asked her why she came back to the Moon. She said she was in a black mood, and the lifelessness of the Moon suited her fine. But she only went out that once. Hovestraydt City isn't lifeless at all, and she wasn't staying in her room all that time either."

"So?"

I didn't have an answer.

Taffy said, "I'll be leaving for Mare Orientale this evening. Marxgrad wants a—"

"Futz!"

"—a surgeon with specialty training in the autonomic muscle system. I can learn a lot there. I'm sorry, Gil."

"Futz, I'm just glad you didn't go yesterday. I'll get drunk with Harry."

"Turn over. Do you want to go to sleep? Here?"

"I don't know what I want. I thought I didn't want to talk."

The lights dimmed. I barely noticed. They brightened again half a minute later, and suddenly I was sitting upright, bug-eyed, sweating.

Taffy said, "The linear accelerator?"

"Yes. She's on her way. When Luke Garner was a boy that flicker would have been the electric chair."

"The what?"

"Skip it."

"Lie down." She went to work on my abdomen. "I don't see why you're quite this shook up. I had the idea she never even slept with you."

"No. Well, once."

"When?"

"About two this morning."

I'd been a little startled when Naomi raised the subject. "I'd have thought sex would be the last thing on your mind."

"But it's our last chance. Unless you wait six months and then buy the appropriate—" She stopped, horrified.

"*Not* funny," I said.

"No. I'm sorry."

"Maybe you'd rather just be held? Cuddled?"

"No." She was out of her dress in an instant. I plucked it out of the wind on its way to the air circulation unit. Then I turned to look at her. I had never seen her naked before. It took my breath away. I caught myself thinking, *Where were you ten years ago, when I needed you?* and was ashamed.

She opened a drawer in the bed table and took out a tube of jell. She was frigid; she was expecting to be frigid; she

kept that tube very handy. This was normal to Naomi.

I couldn't bring her to climax. She faked it very nicely . . . and didn't I owe something to the Gil Hamilton of ten years ago? Wouldn't he have given up a testicle for this night? I made myself enjoy it.

I moved from love into massage. Taffy had taught me massage, both sensual and therapeutic. I managed to relax her, a little. Naomi was on her back, staring at the ceiling while I worked on her hands, when she said, "I'd love to have another baby."

"But you said—"

"Never mind what I said!" Suddenly she was enraged. I turned her over and went back to work, till I had her relaxed again.

We made love, or I did. She couldn't concentrate. I didn't try again. I told her stories from my time in the Belt. She talked about her days in college. She asked about my life as an ARM, and cut me off when I spoke the word *organlegger*. And she kept glancing at the clock.

"What time is it?"

"Oh-eight-ten," Taffy said.

"Time to go to the Conference."

"You're a basket case. I'll call them and tell them you'll make the afternoon session."

"*Oh,* no. Let me make that call. My reputation." I got up. "Chir—"

"Then put some clothes on too," she said sharply.

I got Bertha Carmody, worse luck, and told her the situation. I sat down on the bed, and flopped back, and found my head in Taffy's lap.

I half-woke when a pillow was substituted for the lap.

Then Taffy's phone was saying, "Time to wake up, Ms. Grimes. It's twelve hundred. Time to wake up—"

I called it off, but it wouldn't obey my voice. I swore and rolled off the bed. I should have smashed the phone instead. Or else I should have made the morning session . . .

8.
The Other Crime

The morning session, that fourth day of the Conference, was when they started getting specific about lunar laws. Naomi or no Naomi, I should have been there. By the time Carmody called the afternoon session to order, all I could do was listen and learn what the fighting was about.

Item: death penalties on the Moon included murder, attempted murder, manslaughter, rape, armed theft, theft involving betrayal of trust, and assault. A similar ARM list would have included far more minor crimes, but—

What constituted assault? We ran that around for a good hour. Armed theft and rape were covered by other laws. What about a simple brawl? To Belters, a barroom brawl classed as recreation. Corey Metchikov from Mare Moscoviense explained that lunies were more fragile than Belters *or* flatlanders, and their longer reach gave a fighter extra leverage. A brawl among lunies was *likely* to be lethal, he claimed.

Marion Shaeffer expressed doubt that a lunie had the muscle to hurt even a lunie. Bertha Comody offered to Indian wrestle. Marion accepted. We moved some chairs. They looked ridiculous: Marion wasn't even shoulder high to Bertha. Bertha turned Marion in a complete cartwheel, and it was done purely by leverage.

Stone repeated an earlier demand for a legal definition of rape. That started an uproar. There were statutory penalties to protect minors and the marriage bond, and four outnumbered lunies looked ready for murder or war to preserve them. To Budrys and Shaeffer and Quifting, such laws added up to murder plus invasion of privacy.

I could see their point; but we were *not* here to start a war. I was glad when we got off that subject.

Manslaughter. On the Moon that covered a variety of sins:

sabotage, criminal carelessness, arson— "Any act which, by damaging a local life support system," said Marion Shaeffer, "*could* have caused deaths or injuries. Is that right?"

"Essentially correct," said Ward.

"That goes a little far," said Marion. "*We'd* execute someone who botched repairs on an air recycler if someone died for it. But if nobody actually gets hurt, why not just assess him for damages?"

Ward was on his feet by now, towering over the seated goldskin. "You go a little far yourself," he told her. "Twenty years ago the Moon became the execution grounds for every planet, moon, and rock in the solar system, barring Earth itself. We allowed that. It was a needed source of income. But we will tolerate only limited meddling in our affairs. Beyond that, you may kill your own or ship them to Earth."

Bertha Carmody broke the angry silence. "We're all here to make that step unnecessary. The last Conference left us with a considerable expense in research and construction and maintenance. The holding tanks have cost us well over three billion UN marks to date. We don't *want* to eat the cost. Agreed?"

We looked at each other. At least nobody disagreed.

"Your suggestions, Ms. Shaeffer?"

Marion looked uncomfortable. "I'll make it a motion. Alter the law. Fines for accidental damage to equipment, unless the damage causes death or injury. Anyone who ruins something vital when he can't pay the damage, gets broken up. We can live with that. And I'll move to table the motion till we work up a proposed program of changes."

That passed.

Jabez Stone had some details on the holding tanks and wanted them read into the record. In particular, there had been a power failure at Copernicus in 2111. Four Belt criminals had had to be broken up at once, and almost half the organs had been lost.

"There are safeguards now," Ward told us. "It couldn't happen again. Remember, holding tank technology was somewhat primitive twenty years ago. *We* were made responsible for developing it."

"That's reassuring, but it wasn't what I was getting at. Shouldn't those felons have been revived?"

"They were too badly damaged. Only organs could be saved," Ward told him.

"It bothers me," said Stone. "Never a reversal of sentence. Either this is an admirable record—"

"Stone, for God's sake! Should we have convicted some innocent just to satisfy you by reviving him? Can you name one single sentence which *should* have been reversed?"

Stone said, "Case of Hovestraydt City vs. Matheson & Co. It's in the city computer memory."

And everybody groaned.

If what I needed was something to take my mind off Naomi, then for four days I got my wish.

Days we spent arguing. We spent a full day on Hovestraydt City vs. Matheson & Co., not to mention the night I spent reviewing the case. Allegedly the company's carelessness had contributed to the Blowout of 2107. Two Matheson & Co. employees had gone to the organ banks. Penzler and I got Metchikov to admit in private that they might have been scapegoats, that the case should have been reviewed after the hysteria died down. Publicly, forget it.

Late afternoons I watched the news. Steeping myself in lunar culture was worth a try, but the lunie commentators didn't make it easy. They used unfamiliar slang. They gave excessive detail. They droned.

Evenings I met with Stone and Budrys to discuss policy.

The Belters clearly saw their right, nay, their duty to make the lunar law more humanitarian. The Moon didn't see it that way. I made a long phone call to Luke Garner for instructions. All I could get out of him was that the ARM would support any decision I made.

So I backed Budrys and Stone. To us the lunar law had its peculiarities, but it wasn't unduly harsh. Cultures are entitled to their variety—an attitude you'd expect from a club whose members have been battling with words and weapons and economic pressures for close to two hundred years. The drive that spread mankind through the solar system should have given Belters the same attitude, and I said so during a morning session. It fell flat.

Chris Penzler spoke to me afterward. He wasn't moving like a cripple any more, and some of the foam had sloughed off his chest, leaving bare pink skin bordered by thick black hair. He was a lot more cheerful now. "Kansas boy, you didn't see variety in the Belt. You saw customs different from *Kansas* customs. What would happen to a Belt woman who wanted to raise her children in free fall? How do Belters treat a miner who neglects his equipment? Or a Naderite?" He patted the crown of his head, where what remained of his Belter crest started. "We all cut our hair the same way. Doesn't that tell you something?"

"It should," I admitted. "We Committee members, we're all politicians of a sort, aren't we? Natural meddlers. But what if the UN was meddling with Belt law?"

He laughed. "I don't have to wonder about that—"

"Too right you don't. It happened, and you seceded from Earth! How do you feel about ARM law?"

He told me what I already knew: the laws of Earth made us not much better than organleggers. I said, "Why don't you do something about it?"

"How?"

"Yeah. You don't have the power to pressure Earth. But you think you've got the lunar economy by the throat."

"Gil, I push where I think something will give."

"The Moon might be stronger than you think, or more determined. You could win a war, if it comes to that, but will you like yourselves afterward? And can you keep the UN neutral? Belt ships using asteroids as missiles, we wouldn't like that this close to Earth."

These casual conversations were getting to be more important than the sessions. We took to adjourning in midafternoon. We formed dinner triads: a lunie, a Belter, and a flatlander meeting to seek compromise while full bellies made us mellow. For some of us it worked. Some got indigestion.

A nightmare started me off again.

That fourth day, with three hours to go before dinner with Charles Ward and Hildegarde Quifting, I had gone to my room and flopped on the bed to watch the news.

I remember this item: Mary de Santa Rita Lisboa, the Brazilian planetologist, was doing some excavating south of Tycho. Early that morning she had waded into a dust pool to place some equipment. Her feet grew cold, then numb. She grew frightened almost too late. By the time she reached the edge her legs were frozen to the knees. Before help reached her she had fallen hard enough to break ribs and rip a pinhole leak in her suit. Ten minutes passed before she recognised the pain in her ears for what it was. She had slapped a patch on the gash and kept going, on frozen legs, with both ears and one lung ruined by decompression.

A basically interesting tale, yes? But what I remember is the *patronizing* tone, as if nothing above the level of a plains ape would have done such a damnfool thing. The rest of the news was local, and dull. Presently it put me to sleep.

I shouldn't sleep in the afternoon.

Wandering through a dark, blurred forest, I found Naomi asleep in an ornate twentieth century coffin, the kind with a mattress. I knew just how to wake her. I approached her coffin/bed, bent and kissed her. She fell apart. I tried to put her together with my hands. . .

And woke with questions chasing each other through my head.

. . . Why would anyone lie herself into the organ banks? It was her own business, I told myself; she'd made that clear. But what could she be hiding that would be worth that?

Another crime?

. . . She had phoned me, my first night on the Moon. Why?

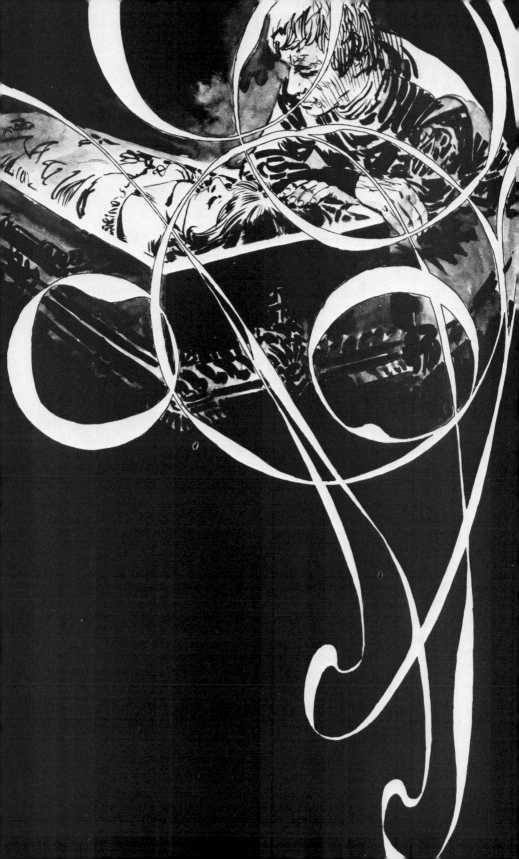

Not because she was eager to see me again. She knew I was an ARM. Was she checking up on me, to see what I suspected?

... She had claimed to be exploring the badlands west of the city. Call that her alibi. Alibi for what? Where could she have gone in four hours, on foot?

I was hooked.

In my copious free time, with ten minutes to go before a dinner session with Charles Ward and Hildegarde Quifting, I tried to call Laura Drury. Her phone told me that she was asleep; please call back after 1230 tomorrow. My answer wasn't recorded, I hope.

Late that night I summoned up a map of the city environs and spent some time studying it.

I called Laura again after the next day's morning session. Laura was in uniform, but she hadn't left her room. I said, "I can't stand the suspense any more. Did Naomi in fact reach a holding tank?"

She blinked. "Of course."

"Is this of your own knowledge?"

"I haven't seen her lying in the tank, no. I'd have heard if there was an escape." She studied my image. "It wasn't just casual sex, was it?"

"I left Earth to mine the asteroids because Naomi married someone else."

"I'm sorry. We tend to think ... I mean ..."

"I know, flatlanders are easy. Have you got a minute to talk?"

"Gil, why don't you stop tormenting yourself?"

"I got to wondering. Naomi was a computer programmer. It was one point against her. The jury assumed she could have got to the message lasers without leaving a record in the computer. Do you believe that?"

"I don't know how good she was. Do you?"

"No. I got to wondering if a computer programmer that good could steal a puffer, again with no records."

She sat down to think. Presently she nodded. "Anyone that good could have stolen a puffer too. No wonder you didn't find the weapon."

"Okay." Though that wasn't exactly what I was after.

"Hold it. With a puffer she could have reached the Belt Trading Post. She could have taken a ship out. Gil, we'd have found her anyway, but at least she would have had a chance! Why would she come back?"

"Yeah, you're right. It was just a thought. Thanks." I called the phone off, and her puzzled frown vanished. Then I started laughing.

Some alibi! And perfectly genuine, too. Naomi could have been committing an entirely different crime at the Belt Trading Post!

I was going to have to walk softly. I would have to find Chris's failed killer *without* showing the lunie police where Naomi actually was.

I was stripping for a bath when Laura called me back that evening. I said, "Chiron, voice only. Hi, Laura, I'm glad you called. Has anything unusual happened lately at the Belt Trading Post?"

"Nothing I've heard about. And there weren't any puffers missing that night."

"What? How sure are you?"

"Mesenchev was on duty. He says there were no puffers checked out, and no slots. No computer program could keep him from noticing one empty slot. And is that finally the end of the Naomi Mitchison case?"

"Yes. And if it isn't, I'll at least quit bugging you. I've done too much of that."

She studied me thoughtfully ... no, she must have been studying a blank screen. She'd better, because I was just climbing into the tub. She said, "Did I louse up a voice-only command a few days ago?"

"Eee-yess. I wasn't about to be the one to tell you."

"Well, you're a gentleman," she said, and called off, leav-

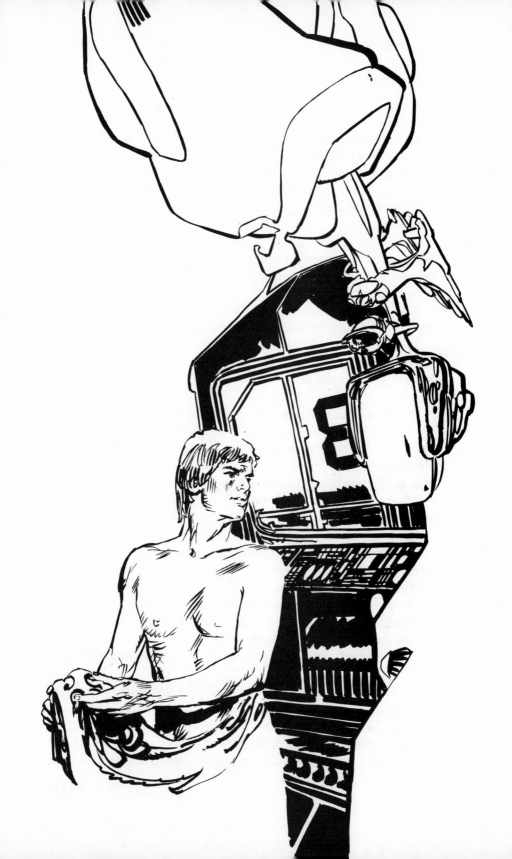

ing me bemused. What did lunies consider a gentleman?

No puffers missing. Futz. While water and air bubbles churned around me, I called up the map again and traced the trade road west. Roads branched off to the water-and-oxygen works, to the abandoned metal mines, to a linear accelerator project that had gone bankrupt.

I was back to assuming Naomi was on foot. Could she have met someone, somewhere within reach? The air works required sunlight. At night they might be deserted. Or what about the old strip mine?

The screen blinked, and Laura Drury glared out of it. "Now, what are you doing with that map again?"

Watery amoebae left the tub with the force of my flinch. "Hey, are you sure that's your business? And how do you break into a computer display without permission, anyway?"

"I knew how to do that when I was ten. Gil, will you give up on her? Maybe she wasn't out there when Penzler got shot. Maybe she researched it somehow. Gil, if she wasn't shooting at Penzler, she must have been committing an organ bank crime somewhere else!"

"You saw that, huh? I went to the wrong person. Well, if you must know, I can't leave puzzles alone."

Long silence. Then, "Want help?"

"Not from a cop. If you found a crime, you'd have to report it."

She nodded reluctantly.

"Hey, why did you call me a gentleman?"

"Well, you didn't ... If a lunie saw a, a person naked on his phone screen—" She stopped.

"He'd crawl out of the screen at you, drooling and leering?"

"He'd think it was an invitation." She was blushing darkly.

"Oh. Hahaha! No. If a lady wants to give me an invitation, I expect her to say so. Flatlanders don't hint." I stood up. "Especially on the Moon. I was told *never* to make advances to a lunie." I started scraping the half-inch of water off me with the edges of my hands. Then I saw her eyes bugging. "Have you got vision?"

She was stricken. *Caught!*

"Serve you right." I reached for a towel. I used it on my hair, concealing my grin, concealing nothing else. Why shouldn't a lunie be curious? And she'd given me the same privilege, inadvertently.

"Gil?"

"Yeah."

"It was an invitation."

I looked at her over the towel. Her lids were lowered and her blush was darker yet.

"Okay, come on up."

"Okay."

It took her forty minutes. She might have been changing her mind over and over again. She arrived still in uniform, carrying a briefcase.

I'd put clothes on, in case anyone was in the hall. Even so, she looked everywhere but at me. Nervous. Her eye caught the phone display.

She studied the map. "On foot, for four hours. Well, what was she doing for four hours?"

"It's like this," I said. "If Naomi wasn't out there shooting at Chris Penzler, then someone else was. We'd both like to find him, right? Because we're cops. But you're a cop, so I can't tell you what I think Naomi was doing."

She sat down stiffly on the edge of the bed. "Say she met someone. Maybe a man who works at the air works. Married. Would she protect him?"

I had to laugh. Naomi? With her *life*? "No. Anyway, what kind of assignation is that? As soon as they take off their clothes, *poof!* Explosive decompression. Laura, how do I go about relaxing you?"

She smiled flickeringly. "Talk to me. This is unusual for me."

"You can change your mind at any second. Just say the word. The word is 'halogens'."

"Thanks."

"Then you have to list them."

A short silence which I had to break. "If she wasn't out there, it makes her useless as a witness, doesn't it? What she swore she didn't see doesn't count. And Chris said there could have been an army out there hiding in the shadows. He wasn't even sure he saw a human being."

She turned to look at me. "That leaves your testimony."

In my mind I flexed my imaginary hand, remembering the feel of miniature moonscape. "There wasn't anyone out

there by the time I looked. Laura, what about mirrors? The laser could have been somewhere else, and the killer too."

"But there wasn't any mirror either."

"I wasn't looking for one."

"We'd have found it."

It was impossible. I scowled at the map. I wanted to ignore the facts and just start toting up suspects according to motive. What stopped me was my first suspect: *any* lunie angry enough about our meddling in lunar affairs, and clever enough to have worked some kind of trickery.

Laura picked up her case and went into the water closet.

I was having trouble keeping my priorities straight. First: I hadn't touched a woman in several days. Second: I didn't want Laura hurt, damaged, or embarrassed. Third: my own part in the Conference could be endangered. Fourth: I wanted Laura Drury in my bed, and that was part lust, part spirit of adventure. How to reconcile all that? Hold it down to talk for now? Let her list her own priorities on her own time?

She came out wearing a garment the likes of which I'd never seen before. It was sexy and strange: floor length, shoulderless, and not quite opaque. The thin, cream-colored fabric hugged her body by static electricity. It could almost have been a dress, but it looked too fragile—there was a lot of lace—and much too thin to hold heat.

"What is it?"

She laughed. "It's a nightgown!" Quite suddenly she came into my arms. I found myself standing fully upright and nuzzling her throat. The garment was nicely tactile: silky smooth over warm skin. I felt her goosebumps through it.

"What's it for?"

"It's to sleep in. For now, I guess it's to take off."

"Carefully? Or do I rip it off?"

"Jesus! Carefully, Gil, it's expensive."

Lunie customs. Sooner or later they'd get me. A sensible man wouldn't have invited a lunie to his room. I knew it and didn't care.

9.
The Trading Post

It was amazing how good we felt on a couple of hours' sleep. Laura was glowing. She kept picking me up in her arms, Rhett Butler style. She'd jump when I goosed her, then steady herself with a hand on my head and let me lift her one-handed. I played tricks with my imaginary arm.

We went formal and cautious when it came time to leave. I left first. Desiree Porter and Tom Reinecke were coming down the hall. They hailed me and swept me up and tried to pump me for news on the Conference.

I sidestepped. "What have you two been doing all this time, just waiting for one of us to crack?"

Tom said, "There was Penzler. There was the trial. We've been interviewing lunies, too. You know, a lot of them aren't going to be happy no matter *what* you do."

"And we screw a lot," Desiree said.

"That I kind of assumed. Hey, did you two know each other before you got here?"

"Nope. It was just one of those things—"

"Lust at first sight. I think it's his legs I like best. Belt men have their muscles mainly in the arms and shoulders."

"So you only love me for my legs, huh?"

"And your mind. Didn't I mention your mind?"

We had reached the elevators. I started to step in, then told them I'd left something in my room, which was true enough.

Now the hall was empty. I called the door open, Laura joined me, and we went down to breakfast. We weren't even holding hands. But our hands brushed sometimes, and Laura kept suppressing a smile, and I wondered just how much we were hiding. For that matter, I'd seen Reinecke's oddly sardonic smile as the elevator doors closed.

At breakfast I told Laura I wanted to check out a puffer. She didn't like it. "Isn't there a Committee meeting?"

"I'll skip a day. Hell, this *is* Committee business. If the courts have convicted an innocent person—"

She shrugged angrily. "If she didn't try to murder Penzler, then she was doing something else!"

The idea percolated through to me that as a man newly

in love, I was supposed to forget old loves entirely. Laura didn't want to hear that I still hoped to save Naomi Mitchison.

I sidestepped again. "I left a case half solved once," I said, and I told her how Raymond Sinclair's surrealistic death scene was linked to two organleggers found with their faces burned down to the bone. I had nearly reached the morgue in the same condition.

Maybe she bought it. She did help me check out a puffer.

The puffers were racked along one wall of the mirror works. Today there were several gaps. The only difference between the orange city police puffers and the rentals was that the rentals came in all colors.

I chose a police puffer. It was a low-slung motorcycle with a wide padded bucket seat and a cargo framework behind. There were three tanks. The motor had no intake. An exhaust pipe forked to left and right just under the seat. The shock absorbers were huge, and the tires were great fat soft tubes.

Laura showed me how to get it going and tried to tell me how to run it, how to maneuver, how to steer, where not to steer. "*I* could cross a dust pool," she told me. "Like a bat out of hell, and if you slow down you'll turn over, and if the wheel hits a submerged rock you'll be under the dust trying to figure out which way is up. You stay away from dust pools. Don't hit any rocks. If you fall, get your arms over your helmet—"

"I'll stick to the road," I said. "That's safe, isn't it?"

"I guess so." She was reluctant to admit that anything was safe.

"Why are there three tanks?"

"Oxygen, hydrogen, water vapor. We don't throw away water, Gil. The exhaust is just a safety valve, and of course it powers the side jets. You shouldn't have to use them, but do it if you think you're falling over."

I climbed on. I could barely feel the vibration. "It isn't puffing," I noticed.

"It's not supposed to. If it starts puffing steam,
something's wrong. That's why they're called puffers. If it
happens, slow way down and check your air, because you
may have to walk home." She insisted on showing me how
to bleed oxygen from the puffer tank into my backpack.

"Have you got all that?"

"Yup."

"Keep it slow till you learn how to steer. This is the Moon.
You'll have to lean further than you think."

"Okay."

"I don't get off till 2000. Will you be back by then?"

"I'm bound to."

We clinked helmets in lieu of a kiss, and I went.

From the city's east face, the mirror works, the trade road
hooked around and aimed straight west. I bounced along at
a fair rate for an off-road vehicle. I marked the tilted rock far
off to my left, and a road that wound uphill to my right, up
to the air and water plant. I had seen it from a height,
miniaturized in the projection room: mirrors mounted
around the rim of a fair-sized recent crater, focussing their
light down onto a pressure vessel filled with red-hot lunar
rock. Pipes to lead hydrogen in, water vapor out. I was
tempted to go up and look at the real thing. Maybe on the
way back...

To my left was the land Naomi had tried to lead us
through, and the peak Naomi had tried to climb. I kept
going.

The road twisted like an injured snake. A broad road led
left toward the strip mines that had made Hovestraydt City
rich. When they played out the city had turned to mirror
making.

Naomi wasn't a native. To meet someone out here, she
would need some obvious landmark. The same would hold
if someone had simply left a puffer parked somewhere for
her. The mines? She couldn't get lost, witnesses were unlikely, and the tailings might fool radar for a small vehicle.

She'd led us a merry dance, the day after the attack on

Chris Penzler. Alan Watson must have given her what she needed when he showed her the projection room. And she'd danced her way right into the organ banks. To hide what?

Or else the jury was right.

Presently I was bouncing downhill, beyond the region I'd searched with my imaginary hand, beyond anywhere Naomi could have reached on foot. Far ahead was a line of silver: the mass driver built to supply ore for the L-5 project of the 2040s. The company had gone bankrupt, and the mass driver was half built and long obsolete.

I kept checking my watch.

There was the Trading Post ahead. Unused to picking out details in moonscape, my eyes had been missing it for some time. I found the shapes of two spacecraft first, then the outline of the spaceport, then the crescent of stone-and-glass buildings around it. The road became a circle between the buildings and the spaceport. I had made the run in just thirty-five minutes.

The Trading Post was strange by anyone's standards.

There was no dome. Oblong buildings were individually pressurized; sometimes they were linked by tunnels. In Selene's Bar and Grill, where I stopped for lunch, I found racks for fishbowl helmets but none for pressure suits. The customers kept their credit coins in outside pockets.

Selene's Bar and Grill, Mare Serenitatis Spa (with a pool and sauna), the Man in the Moon Hotel (he was shown yawning), Aphrodite's: all the place names were moon-related. Half the people I saw were lunies. Aphrodite's rented sexual favors. The waitress at Selene's told me it catered specifically to lunies. I was a little shocked.

The administration building was all the way around the circle. It was big enough to get lost in. The police, licensing, and port administration were scattered through the building. I finally found the goldskin offices.

"ARM business," I told the only clerk in sight.

He was watching a fold-up 3D screen propped in front of him. He didn't look up. "Yah?"

"Last Wednesday someone shot a Belt delegate to the Conference on—"

Now he looked up. "We heard about that. Didn't they solve that one? I heard—"

"Look, there's a possibility that our suspect was *here* at the time. That would mean she wasn't shooting at Penzler. We never found the weapon either. That adds up to a would-be killer with a message laser still hunting a Belt delegate."

"See your point. What do you need?"

"Were there any crimes committed here between 2230 Tuesday and 0130 Wednesday?" Naomi would have had to walk to where someone left a puffer for her, then drive here. At least half an hour coming and half an hour back. Later I'd have to pace it off on foot.

He set aside his fold-up screen and tapped at a computer keyboard. The screen lit. "Mmm ... we had a fight at Aphrodite's about that time. A lunie dead, two Belters and a lunie under arrest, all male. But you're looking for something premeditated."

"Right."

"Zip."

"Futz. How about disappearances?"

He summoned up the Missing Persons records. Nobody had been reported missing since Wednesday. It seemed that Naomi had not been committing a crime of violence.

"How well do you keep track of your puffers?"

"They're licensed. Generally the residents own their own." He was typing as he spoke. The screen filled. "These are rentals—"

"*Chili Bird?*" The name rang a bell.

"Two puffers charged to the *Chili Bird* account for two days. Well, that's reasonable. Antsie had passengers."

"Tell me more."

He scowled—I was inventing work for him, and he would have preferred not to—but he typed, and more data appeared. "Antsie de Campo, owner and pilot of *Chili Bird* out of Vesta. Arrived April 10. Left April 13. Passengers, Dr. Raymond Forward and a four-year-old girl, Ruth Hancock

Cowles. Cargo ... he had a light load. Monopoles. He took off with some chicken and turkey embryos; maybe that's why the doctor was along."

April 13 was the day after the attempt on Penzler. "Where are they now?"

"Headed for Confinement Asteroid. Probably because of the little girl." He typed. "I remember her now. She was a doll. Interested in everything. She loved low gravity; she was bouncing around—" The screen responded. "*Chili Bird*'s almost to Confinement now. Is this any use to you?"

"I hope so. Where can I send a message to *Chili Bird*?"

He told me how to find Interplanetary Voice, on a peak outside the city circle.

There would have been several minutes' lightspeed delay in conversation. I sent a straight 'gram.

TO: DR RAYMOND FORWARD

NAOMI MITCHISON TRIED AND CONVICTED FOR AT-TEMPTED MURDER COMMITTED HOVESTRAYDT CITY 0130 WEDNESDAY APRIL 13. EXECUTION PENDING. IF YOU KNOW OF HER MOVEMENTS DURING RELEVANT TIME, CALL ME HOVESTRAYDT CITY.

GILBERT HAMILTON, ARM

I didn't stop on the way home. I couldn't guess where someone might have left a puffer for Naomi. Maybe I had already wasted time I couldn't afford. I felt time's hot breath on the back of my neck, an unreasonable conviction that Naomi didn't have months, but only hours.

McCavity hailed me in the hall. "Hello, Gil. The offer's still open," he said.

"Offer?"

"Someone to get drunk with."

"Oh. I may need it yet. Let me buy you a drink now. I haven't seen a bar—"

"There aren't any. We tend to keep our own supplies and drink in our rooms. Come on, I've got a good stock."

McCavity's quarters were near the bottom level of the city.

He didn't have any kind of bartending device; the drinks were going to be simple. He offered me something he called *earthshine* poured over ice, and I took it.

Smooth.

"Distilling is dirt cheap here," Harry said. "Heat, cold, partial vacuum, they're all just outside the wall. Do you like it?"

"Yeah. It tastes like a good bourbon."

"I got a call from Taffy. She reached Marxgrad okay. She says she left you a message too."

"Good."

"I gather you got together okay?"

"Yes, thank God. I was a basket case. She reassembled me." I sipped again. "I wish I had the time to get drunk in good company. It might be just what I need. Harry, do you know of a Belt doctor, a Raymond Forward?"

McCavity scratched his head. "Rings a bell. Yeah, he's got some lunie clients. Specialist in fertility problems."

Futz. Naomi didn't suffer from infertility. "He was on the Moon for a few days. Maybe he had a lunie client?"

"There'd be records. We don't have restrictions on fertility, except the natural ones."

"Okay, I can check that out."

"What's it all about?"

"He was here at the right time, and he came in with a light cargo. Maybe there were ulterior motives."

"Right time for what?"

"Naomi. Maybe I'm going at this wrong end round. I should be looking for whoever shot at Chris Penzler. But if Naomi wasn't where she said she was . . . well, it's one handle on a puzzle. I can track that down. She could have been meeting someone. Maybe Antsie de Campo, maybe Forward. Could there be two Raymond Forwards?"

"Both Belt doctors? Well, it's possible." He sipped at his own drink. "Was Naomi infertile?"

"She was fertile. She'd also sworn never to have another kid."

"Then *that's* out."

"By another man."

"What?"

"She swore she'd never have children by another man. This Forward, he solves infertility problems?"

"Right. You've got something, don't you?"

"Cloning?"

"If all else fails, he can grow a clone for a patient. It's hellishly expensive."

"Can I borrow your phone?"

"I'll call for you. What number?"

I told him.

Artemus Boone stood frowning in the doorway of his office. "I was just closing up. I can meet you tomorrow at 1000. Unless it's urgent?"

"It feels urgent," I told the phone image. "Do you still regard Naomi Mitchison as your client?"

"Certainly."

"I need to discuss her case, confidentially."

He sighed. "Come to my office. I'll wait."

I turned to Harry McCavity. "Thanks for the drink. I'll be pleased to get drunk with you when this is all over, but just now—"

He waved that off. "Will I ever know what this was all about?"

"There's more than one kind of crime," I said cryptically, and left.

Artemus Boone sat behind his ancient, lovingly maintained computer terminal and propped his beard on his folded hands. "Now, what's this all about, Mr. Hamilton?"

"I want a legal opinion on a hypothetical situation."

"Go on."

"A flatlander woman hires a Belt doctor to take a clone from her and grow it to term. The operation takes place on the Moon. The woman returns to Earth. The child is raised in the asteroids. Four years later they meet again, on the

Moon. The woman is still on the Moon when it all becomes public knowledge."

Boone stared as if I'd sprouted horns. "Damnation!"

"Sure. Now, the United Nations Fertility Laws would have our hypothetical flatlander woman sterilized if she had an illegal baby. They'd sterilize the baby too. But this particular woman still has one birthright, so she could have a baby with no problem. But what about a clone?"

Boone shook his head. He was still thunderstruck. "I don't know. My field is lunar law."

"Would the UN try to extradite the woman? Would the Moon let them get away with it? Would they try to extradite the baby too? Or are they both safe because the crime took place off Earth?"

"Again, I don't know. I'd want to research this. In some legal respects the Moon is part of the United Nations. Damnation! Why didn't she discuss this with me?"

"She could have been scared to. She never mentioned any such situation?"

He smiled like a man in pain. "Never. Damnation. I'm nearly certain that the baby could not be extradited. If only she'd asked! Hamilton, is our hypothetical baby still on the Moon?"

"No."

"Good." He stood up abruptly. "I'll be able to give you a better answer tomorrow. Call me."

I reached my room expecting to spend some time on the phone. Getting Budrys to tell me what went on at the Conference could take up to an hour. I wanted to check Dr. Forward's credentials and recent movements. And Taffy's message was waiting . . . I dropped onto the bed and pulled my shoes off and said, "Chiron, messages."

And Laura Drury's image, in full pressure suit, said, "Gil, you'll have to have dinner without me. I'm going out with a search party. I don't know when I'll be back. Chris Penzler's turned up missing."

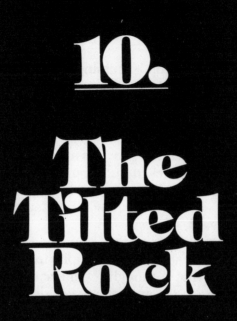

10.

The Tilted Rock

I wasted a few seconds cursing. The urgency I'd felt hadn't been for Naomi Mitchison. Naomi was feeling no impatience. Death had been hunting Chris Penzler.

I called Laura's room and got no answer. I called the police and got Jefferson.

"He left about sixteen twenty this afternoon," the freckled lunie told me. "He checked out a puffer."

I said, "Idiot."

"Right. How well do you know him? Could he think he's playing detective?"

"Why not? Somebody wants him dead, and it bothers him. He's not likely to be out there playing tourist."

"Well, that's what I thought," Jefferson said. "I sent a search party west, to the area where Penzler testified he saw something. Laura Drury's with them, in case you were wondering." A trace of disapproval in his voice. What the futz? "But they haven't found him, and they've been out over an hour."

"Set the area up in the projection room and search that."

"We have *got* to have another Watchbird satellite," Jefferson said. "There used to be three. The replacement keeps getting proxmired in the budget hearings. Hamilton, we've been waiting for the Watchbird One to rise. Why don't you meet me down in the projection room?"

"Good."

Tom Reinecke and Desiree Porter were waiting outside the projection room. They'd heard Chris Penzler was missing. Jefferson wanted to tell them to go to hell until I said, "We can use some extra eyes."

Yet again we waded out into the hologram, knee deep in miniature moonscape. Jefferson and Reinecke and I fanned out into the choppy lands west of the rim wall and the city. Porter searched the crater itself, because nobody else had. Partly to honor her theory, I stopped at the tilted rock.

Jefferson and Tom Reinecke kept going. They glanced back at me, then resumed their search by eye alone, three to four hundred yards from the west wall of the city.

I looked around. The tilted rock was small enough to heft in both arms, except that it wouldn't have moved, of course. I saw tiny orange suits with bubble helmets scattered over the rocks to my west. I called, "What kind of suit would Chris be wearing?"

"Blue, skintight, with a gold and bronze griffon on the chest," Jefferson called back.

There were annoying blank spots in the landscape, where the Watchbird's cameras weren't reaching. I tried to feel around in them, but my talent wasn't up to that. I felt nothing.

I found no blue skintight suits, vertical or horizontal. Where Reinecke and Jefferson were searching, bright orange puffers were parked in a ring on flat ground. None in my area.

There was a deep dust pool twenty yards south of the tilted rock. The surface looked roiled. I ran my imaginary hand beneath the surface, and flinched violently. Then I made myself touch it again.

I called, "I've found the puffer. It's under the dust."

One and all, they abandoned their own search. Desiree reached me first. They watched (for what?) while I let go of the puffer and searched further. I found it almost at once. I said, "God."

Desiree said, "What? Penzler?"

I closed my hand around it. It felt light and dry, like a dead lizard left in the sun. "Somebody. A suit with somebody inside." I made my imaginary fingertips follow the contours of the thing, though there was nothing less I wanted in the world. "God. His hand is gone."

My hand stopped sending. My talent had quit. Imaginary hand, hell; it's my mind, my unprotected mind, that feels out the textures of what I touch. I can only take so much of that.

"We'll have to check this out," Jefferson said.

"Use your belt phone. Send the search party that way. Tell

them we'll join them as soon as we can."

It took almost an hour. I was twitchy with impatience. When we finally set forth, our team included Jefferson, both newstapers, dredging machinery and a couple of orange-clad operators.

The Earth was a broad crescent, not quite half full. The sun was well up the sky, leaving fewer shadows, but these were impenetrably black. Our headlamps didn't help. Our bubble helmets had darkened and our eyes had adjusted to lunar day.

The dozen cops on the original search team were already waiting at the dust pool. Laura Drury bounced up to me. "Do you really think he's down there?"

"I felt him," I said.

She grimaced. "Sorry. Well, we found this. It was just under the dust, just at the edge." She held an elastic strap with a buckle, the kind that locks when you pull it tight. "We use them on puffers, to hold small stuff on the frame behind the seat. Does it mean anything to you?"

"Not a thing," I said.

"Maybe the killer dumped the body in the dust," Laura speculated, "and then found the strap. He just stuck it under the dust with his hand."

That would mean he was in a hurry, I thought. It would also mean the strap was evidence of something. Otherwise he'd have just kept it.

Jefferson called Laura, and she waved and went.

I noticed Alan Watson by his height. While the cops were getting the equipment ready, Alan and I adjusted our radios for privacy.

"I've got news," I said. "Maybe good, maybe bad."

"About Naomi?"

"Right. She wasn't here when someone shot Penzler in his bath. She wasn't anywhere near here. She was at the Belt Trading Post."

"Then she's innocent! But why wouldn't she say so?"

"She thought she was committing an organ bank crime."

Alan's face twisted. "That isn't a whole lot of help."

The dredge moved into the dust, sinking. The dust was deep. I'd felt it.

"It could help," I said. "We have to prove that someone else tried to shoot Chris, without showing what Naomi was actually doing. Then we could get her revived."

"By God, we could! If that's Penzler down there, then the original assassin got him."

"Maybe not. His methods seem to have turned crude. We'd still want to show how he could fire a laser at Chris Penzler's window from out here and then get back into the city, or wherever he did go, and why I didn't find him in the projection room. And after all, that might not even be Penzler's body. All I know is, there's someone down there."

"Um."

"What I'd rather do is show that what Naomi was doing *wasn't* an organ bank crime. She should've discussed it with her lawyer. What I think she—"

The dredge came out of the dust, and I dropped the conversation and loped over.

The corpse wore a blue skintight suit. The right hand had been sliced off cleanly, four inches above the wrist. The face seemed shrunken, but I would have recognised him even without the torso painting, the Bonnie Dalzell griffon clutching Earth in its claw.

I opened my radio band and announced, "It's Chris Penzler."

Jefferson examined the severed forearm. "Clean cut. Message laser on high," he said. "The beam must have sliced right through. If there was rock behind him, we'll find the marks." He set some of the cops to searching.

We didn't bother to look for bootprints. The search party had left too many. But they hadn't left puffer tracks. We found a set of puffer tracks and followed them backward from the pool until they disappeared on bare rock.

Someone behind us announced that he had found the hand. Jefferson went back. I didn't. Those tracks could lead from the general direction of the tilted boulder.

Six nights ago, Chris Penzler had glimpsed someone through his picture window. Only for an instant ... and afterward he couldn't decide which side of this particular boulder he'd been looking past. Maybe he'd come out to see.

The flat side of the rock was in deep shadow. I stepped close to the rock, out of the sun, and waited for my darkened helmet to clear again and my eyes to adjust. Then I played my headlamp over the rock.

My yell brought them running. They clustered around me to look at Chris Penzler's dying message: big, malformed letters scrawled across the rock, black in the light of the headlamps.

NAKF

"He must have written it in his own blood," Jefferson said. "In shadow, so the killer wouldn't notice. He must have been jetting blood from the severed artery. But ... that isn't a name, is it?"

Desiree said, "It isn't anything. I think."

"The strap!" Laura cried in the joyful tones that go with the *Eureka!* sensation. "The strap, he must have used it for a tourniquet! He must have known he was dying—maybe he had to hide from the killer—" Her voice dropped. "It's *awful*, isn't it?"

"Take a scraping of that blood," Jefferson ordered. "At least we'll find out if it was Penzler's. He must have had *something* in mind."

I got back to my room around midnight. I set it up on my phone screen:

NAKF

So here's Chris Penzler out there on the meteor-torn moon, looking for clues. Maybe he remembers something. Maybe he finds something. Maybe not.

But a killer finds him.

A lunie citizen would be more likely to know it when Chris Penzler checked out a puffer. Assume he followed immediately ... on foot, unless he was an idiot. I'd ask the computer if someone checked out a puffer right after Chris

did. Some killers *are* idiots.

If Christ had recognised his killer he'd have written a name. I'd get the computer to search the city directory. Offhand I didn't know anyone on the Moon whose name started with NAKF. Or with—I started filling in letters. Written in haste in jetting blood, and possibly in darkness, a *K*

could be a ruined *R*, *F* could be *E*, *N* could be *M* or *W*...
NARF NAKE NARE MAKF MAKE MARE WAKF WAKE
WARE

No names sprang to mind. And Chris wasn't a lunie; here on the Moon I knew everyone he did.

NAKF NAOMI

It was a bad fit. And Naomi had one hell of an alibi. I should be able to persuade the lunar law to disgorge her on the strength of Penzler's murder. If there were indeed two killers after Chris's blood—Naomi the clumsy one, somebody else the skillful or lucky or more straightforward one —Naomi could be returned to the holding tank.

I called, "Chiron, phone. Get me Alan Watson." And my nasty suspicious mind gave me:

NAKF ALAN WATSON WATS

Alan was out on the Moon at the time, in the search party looking for Chris Penzler himself. So maybe he found him. How much would Alan do for Naomi? Would he murder a stranger who had done her harm, if it would buy her life?

Alan's long black-browed face appeared. On the phone screen he was easier to take; his height didn't show. "Hello, Gil."

An N could be a W with the first vertical botched; but an F could not be a botched S, I decided. I said, "I wondered if we can get Naomi out of Copernicus now."

"I've already filed with the court. All we can do now is wait. I expect they'll revive her, but it would help if we could tell them where she actually was. Gil, where was she?"

"I should know that within a few hours." I didn't add that I might not tell him then...

Assume Chris didn't recognise his killer. He couldn't give us a name if all he saw was a pressure suit. Short, medium, or lunie? Inflated or skintight? Chris hadn't bothered to tell us. Could he have had something more specific in mind? Like a torso painting?

Lunch was a long time in the past. I had seen corpses uglier than Chris Penzler's. Maybe I could have done something to save his life . . . but I still had no idea what it might be. I phoned down for a chicken-and-onion sandwich.

Then I put the display back on the phone screen and stared at it.

He must have known he was dying. He'd have kept it short. Unless I was overlooking some significance to NAKF, he had *still* run out of time or blood.

Try NAKE, then. SNAKE? But if I made the F an unfinished E, then he wasn't writing backward. And why should he? So try

NAKF NAKED

For a torso painting? That wouldn't help much. Naked ladies were very popular as torso paintings . . . in the Belt, at least.

Try something else. Picture a vindictive, dedicated killer tracking Chris across the moon, bare-assed but for his trusty laser . . . taking his vengeance just before internal pressure rips him apart in a gust of cold scarlet fog . . . no? Then how about a vehicle with a transparent bubble cockpit? Park it in shadow, with the cockpit lights on, and Chris would see only the killer. But I didn't know of any such vehicle. A custom job? And it would have shown on radar if it flew, would have left tracks if it didn't.

I tried some other words—

My door announcer said, "Gil, are you there? It's Laura."

"Chiron, door open."

She'd showered away the sweat secretions that accumulate on your skin when you're in a pressure suit. I hadn't. Suddenly I felt grimy. She said, "We've made a little progress. I thought you'd want to know."

"What have you got?"

She sat down on the bed beside me, comfortably close. "Nobody checked out a puffer after Penzler did. Not till the search party went out. That puts our killer on foot. It would slow him down."

"Maybe. Maybe he can get a puffer without leaving a computer record. Wouldn't he have to do that to get at the lasers?"

"Um."

"Or if he was a cop with the search party, that would get him the puffer and the laser too."

She scowled.

"Skip it. What have you got on the body?"

"Harry McCavity's doing an autopsy outside the mirror works. The condition of the body ... well, it's freeze-dried. Harry got positively nasty when I wanted a time of death. And the tanks bled empty within half an hour, and his watch didn't conveniently stop either."

"Laura, can I ask you some questions about lunar customs?"

She looked down at me. "Go ahead."

"I already know that people here are supposed to share a bed only when they're married to each other. What I want to know is, if two unmarried people *did* share a bed, would they be expected to share a bed only with each other?"

Her voice turned brittle, and she sat very straight on the bed. "What started you on this?"

"I've been getting some funny vibrations." I didn't name Jefferson.

"Yes. Well. I haven't been bragging about the short, strong fellow I managed to entrap, if *that's* what you're thinking. I don't know how anyone would know about us."

"Maybe lunies tend to know each other better than flat-landers do. Smaller population. Smaller cities. And there *is* such a thing as telepathy." And Laura had been smiling and sparkling as we left her apartment this morning. Someone might have noticed.

"What is it you want to know? Should you resume your relationship with Dr. Grimes? Did you think you needed my permission?"

"I think there are five lunies I don't want to offend," I said. "You, and four Committee delegates from four lunar cities. If you and I are now supposed to be monogamous, I want to know it. I came to the Moon largely because Taffy was here. Should I now stop seeing Taffy in private? Or at all? Come on, give me some help. If the Committee is too busy

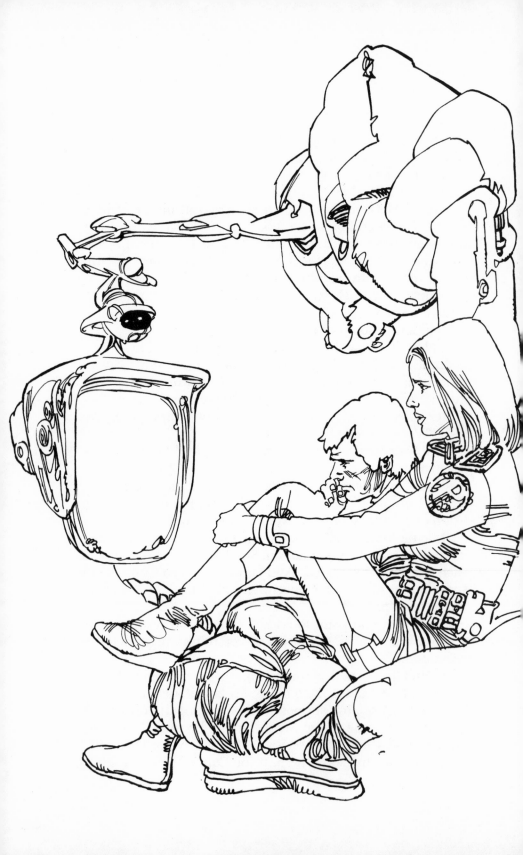

fighting to make decisions, everybody loses."

She screwed her eyes almost shut. "This is all new to me. Let me think." Pause. "I want you for myself. Is that immoral?"

"Depends on where you are. Silly but true. I am flattered."

"All right. Stop seeing her in *public*." By now she was on her feet and pacing like a tiger. "Even in the halls. In private, make *sure* it's private. No phone calls. No room service breakfast for two."

"Taffy's gone to Marxgrad."

"What?"

"She's got her own career to pursue. Now she's pursued it to the back of the Moon. But I had to know these things for future reference, Laura. Are you angry?"

She looked at me. She turned to the door. I said, "Remember, I'm likely to believe anything you tell me. Call me ignorant. Are you angry? Shall we avoid each other from now on?"

She turned back. "I'm angry. I made the same mistake anyone else would have. I want you back in my bed as soon as I get *over* this!" She swung around to the door, and back again. Hesitated. Finally, she dropped back on the bed just behind my shoulder.

It wasn't me that had stopped her, I think. It was the display.

<pre>
                    N A K F
   NARF NAKE NARE MAKF MAKE MARE WAKF
                 WAKE WARE
          N A K F   N A O M I
          N A K F   W A T S
      N A K E D   S N A K E   S N A R E   W A K E N
</pre>

"See anything?"

"Beware?"

I said, "He'd have to add on at both ends."

"That applies to M's and W's too. Oh, I see. If he missed a stroke right at the beginning—"

"Yeah. Do lunies tend to put nudes in their torso paintings?"

"No."

"Do lunies use any kind of vehicle with a *lot* of glass in it? A full bubble cockpit? Do the Belters at the Trading Post?"

"I don't think so. Why?"

"NAKED. And now I'm stuck. Futz. Maybe he was trying to describe a torso painting?"

Laura said, "He must have got away from the killer. Maybe he ducked into the shadows and tied a tourniquet and kept going. Otherwise it's too easy for the killer. A second swipe with the laser cuts him in half."

"Maybe. What's your point?"

"He knew he'd die when he took the tourniquet off. He would have thought it through in detail before he wrote any message." She studied the screen. She reached past me and typed:

Na K F

"Chemistry. Sodium, potassium, flourine."

"What does it mean? What do you do with those three elements?"

"*I* don't know. Gil—"

The door announcer said, "Room service."

Laura yelped. In an instant she was behind the door, flattened against the wall. I stared. Then I went to the door, called it open, stepped into the hall and took the tray, said, "Thank you. Good night," and closed the door in the bemused waiter's face.

Laura exhaled.

I was trying not to laugh. I took a huge bite out of a sandwich and spoke around it. "I need a bath almost as much as I need food. I'm hoping you'll stay; I'm just telling you."

"I'll do your back," Laura said.

"Good."

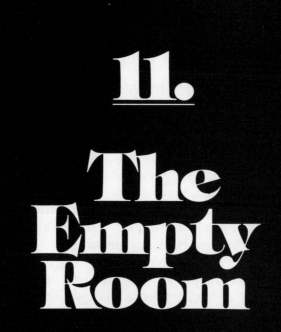

11.

The Empty Room

I was half awake. My mind, idling in neutral, played word games.

NAKF LAURA DRURY DESK COP NAKF

I couldn't make it fit.

Laura's foot was hooked under mine. When she tried to turn over I came fully awake. I worked my foot free and she rolled just to the edge of the bed.

NAKF ... DRURY ... what the *hell* was I doing?

Properly horrified, I pushed the whole topic way down to the bottom of my mind and left it there. But I couldn't get back to sleep. I finally moved to the foot of the bed and said, "Chiron, low volume. Chiron, messages."

Taffy looked good, brisk and happy. "I like Marxgrad," she said. "I like the people. I'm brushing up on my medical Russian, but everyone speaks enough English for social purposes. I miss you mostly at night.

"I hope you haven't changed your mind about having children. I can find the time starting a year from now. We do have a problem. Neither of us intends to drop his career, right? And we're both subject to emergency calls. That could be tough on children."

Another complication I hadn't dealt with yet.

"So think it over," the recording said. "We may want to go into a multiple marriage. Think about the people we know. Is there anyone we can both stand to live with for the first, oh, five to ten years? For instance, how do Lila and Jackson Bera feel about children? Do you know? Think it over and then call me. My love to you and Harry," she said, and was gone.

Laura was watching me. She started to say something, but the next message beat her to it.

The picture was fuzzy. Two men and a laughing little blond girl floated in free fall, at skew angles. The man holding the little girl's hand was a rotund, cheerful man with thick white hair. The other was short and dark and very round of face, partly or wholly Eskimo, I guessed. I didn't know any of them.

"I am Howard de Campo, called Antsie, citizen of Vesta,"

the smiling Eskimo said. "You called to be informed of the motions of Mrs. Naomi Mitchison during certain hours. From 2250 Tuesday to 0105 Wednesday, the lady in question was in *Chili Bird* visiting I and my passenger, Dr. Raymond Q. Forward. The purpose of the visit is secret, but we will tell if necessary, of course. If you have to know more, call us at Confinement, please." The picture blinked out.

"By God, you were right," Laura said. "I could probably even guess the crime."

"They haven't admitted anything," I said. But the blond, blue-eyed little girl must have been included deliberately. She was Naomi at age four.

Laura said, "'Love to you and Harry.' No lunie could ever have said that."

"She meant it."

"Suppose she'd known I was listening?"

"Would you object to my telling her, some day?"

"Please don't," said Laura. She controlled it well, but the idea upset her. "Are you thinking of having children by Taffy Grimes?"

"Yes."

"What about us?"

I hadn't thought of that at all. "I wouldn't be here to act like a father. And I'll be sterile for another four months. Anyway, would my genes be right?"

"I didn't mean . . . never mind." She rolled over and came into my arms. The rest of our conversation was nonverbal. But what *had* she meant?

Shaeffer and Quifting had called Ceres to ask that a third Belter be chosen and sent to the Moon as quickly as possible. Meanwhile the Conference would continue without Chris Penzler.

A nervous urgency was apparent while we were still involved with coffee and rolls. Charles Ward tried to assure us, before anyone else had suggested the possibility, that Chris had *not* been murdered by local terrorists bent on disrupting or exterminating the Conference. The other lunies were quick to agree. Sure. Where were they getting their data?

Just before 0900, I phoned the Mayor's office from the Conference room. "You've heard about Chris Penzler?"

"Yes. A very sticky situation, Gil." The Mayor was perturbed, and it showed. "We're doing all we can, of course. I imagine this will disrupt the Conference."

"We'll see. That might have been the whole idea. Has Naomi Mitchison been released from the holding tanks?"

"No."

"Why not?"

"Releasing a convict from a holding tank isn't done by a wave of the hand. The medical—"

"Mayor, your holding tanks aren't that different from the ones on the slowboats, the interstellar colony ships. Crew members go in and out of the holding tanks a dozen times during any trip."

Hove's eyes flicked past my shoulder. I glanced back and found that I had an audience. Several Conference members were following our conversation. That was all to the good, I thought.

Hove was saying, "You know nothing about the medical complexities. Furthermore, Mrs. Mitchison is a convicted criminal. Reversal of her sentence will not be accomplished by a wave of the hand either."

"In that case, I'm going to raise some hell," I said.

"How do you mean that?"

I said, "The proceedings of the Conference have been confidential so far—"

"And should be!" Bertha Carmody barked in my ear.

"Futz, Bertha, this is at the heart of what's been blocking us all along! Mayor, there's some question as to whether your law gives adequate protection to the defendant. Trials are over almost before they begin, and in twenty years not one sentence has been reversed. Naomi Mitchison's trial is the first to be investigated by outsiders. We now have evidence that someone else wanted Chris Penzler dead all along. Your son has filed to obtain Mrs. Mitchison's release. But when a Committee member, me, checks with the Mayor

of Hovestraydt City, it turns out the conviction isn't even under review!"

"Damn it, Gil, the conviction *is* under review, right now!"

"Good. How long would you expect it to take?"

"I have no idea. A reversal may have to wait until the new investigation is over."

"Fine. In the meantime, get her out of the holding tank."

"Why? Chris's death may be unrelated to the first attempt."

"Granted. I won't try to guess the odds. I'll put it to you that Naomi is likely innocent—"

"Likely is too strong a word."

"—*and* a possible witness. Aside from that, the Committee may want to call her to testify firsthand on how she's been treated. We've examined exactly two trials under lunar jurisprudence, and the other one ... ah—"

"Matheson and Company," Stone put in helpfully.

"Yeah. That one looks kind of funny, too. And Naomi is still in a holding tank waiting to be broken up. How will all of this look to the newstapers?"

Bertha roared, "These proceedings are confidential! Hamilton, how can you think of exposing our deliberations to the news media?"

I said, "All right, Bertha. I'll stick to my opinions on the Mitchison case."

"I hope that that will not be necessary," the Mayor said. "I intend to order Naomi Mitchison revived at once. She will be returned here under arrest, to play her part in the investigation into Chris Penzler's death. Is *that* satisfactory, Mr. Hamilton?"

"Yes. Thank you." I called off the phone, and Bertha called the meeting to order.

When we broke for lunch, I suited up and headed for the mirror works. I found Harry McCavity just outside the airlock, waiting for it to cycle.

"I'm beat," he said. "It's been a long night. Morning, Gil ... no, let me show you something first, and then I'm for bed."

He led me through the mirror works. "Penzler died from loss of blood," he said. "He was wearing a skintight suit. Cutting his hand off didn't release the pressure on his skin. But the blood must have jetted like a fire hose."

"He used it to write with."

"Drury told me. He'd have had to write *fast*."

Penzler's corpse was outside, in vacuum, under a silvered canopy to keep it cold. The dry remains had been sliced to obtain cross sections. They looked like petrified wood. Penzler's skintight pressure suit was next to it, opened along the back and spread like a pelt. The golden griffon glowed on its chest.

Harry picked up Chris's hand, a withered brown claw with four inches of wrist attached. He held it against the severed forearm. What with the shrinking of the flesh, it was hard to tell whether they belonged together. "Look at the bones," he said.

The ends of the bones were quite smooth and fitted perfectly.

"And here." He picked up the right glove from the pressure suit. "His hand was in it. Now look." He held it against the sliced fabric of the pressure suit's forearm.

There was almost no material missing. The laser had sliced through cleanly, at very high energy density, and no thicker than a fishing leader. Even laser beams spread with distance. "They must have been close together when it happened," I said.

"Too right. Penzler and his killer couldn't have been more than three feet apart."

"Huh." I tried to scratch my head through the helmet. "Harry, I don't know what it means yet."

We went back inside, and Harry headed for his bed. I called Artemus Boone and got him to join me for lunch.

We moved down the buffet table collecting dollops and samples of everything in sight. The food on Boone's plate became a precariously balanced cone with a hard boiled pigeon's egg at the apex. He lowered it to the table slowly, with both hands.

"It's not bad," he told me. "It's only complicated. I could argue either way: that Mrs. Mitchison is subject only to the lunar law, or only to United Nations law, whichever she likes."

"So?"

"United Nations law would sterilize her, I think. She is both the father and mother. One could argue that she has used two birthrights. Sterilization wouldn't stop her from growing another clone, so she might not object. For the same reason, the law might demand the right to execute her, but I think I could block that."

"How sure are you?"

"Not very. UN law isn't my home turf. I'd rather work within lunar law. As for the child, she can't be extradited, but she should never visit Earth."

"What's the position under lunar law?"

"Lunar law includes nothing like your fertility quotas. Women who bear children without previous marriage are on their own unless the father sues for his rights ... well, that doesn't apply. But de Campo and Mrs. Mitchison *have* violated lunar medical restrictions. I'd think we want to stand trial here, then claim double jeopardy before the UN."

"She'd be safe then?"

"Up to a point." Boone coughed delicately. "The lady's attitude toward men might hamper her popularity with a jury. And there is still the matter of an attempted murder charge."

"Yeah. I need to talk about the murder," I said, "and I've run out of people to talk with. Have you got some free time?"

"Some. You don't propose to solve both crimes yourself, this afternoon, do you?"

"Why not?"

Boone smiled. "Why indeed? For my defense of Mrs. Mitchison I needed a suspect other than Mrs. Mitchison. My main obstacle was your testimony."

"I can't change it. There wasn't anyone else out on the Moon, and no message laser."

"Well?"

"I keep thinking in terms of mirrors. Boone, I wish to Hell I could put a mirror out there. That way the killer and the weapon could both be somewhere else."

Boone had been eating, talking between mouthfuls. He had a voracious appetite for so lean a man. He chewed and thought, and swallowed, and said, "But the mirror would have to be in place."

"Remember how Chris acted when we asked him what kind of pressure suit the killer was wearing? He sweated. He dithered. He said he might have seen an optical illusion."

"A terrible experience. He might have blocked the memory."

"Sure. Then six days later he left us a dying message. Do you know about that?"

"N A K F. Meaningless."

"I've been assuming he died before he could finish. What was he trying to tell us? NAKED?"

"On the Moon?" Boone smiled.

"Naked to vacuum," I said. "Chris stood up in his bath and saw someone out on the Moon without a pressure suit. Don't you see, he was looking in a mirror."

"But what was he seeing? Himself?"

"No. He saw the killer. The killer must have been in one of the other apartments. Poor Chris, he must have thought he was going crazy. No wonder he wouldn't talk about it."

Boone ate quietly for a time. Then he said, "Mrs. Mitchison was on the second floor. We tend to put outworlders on the ground floor. Were all the ground floor apartments full? This is something we can check, but you see the implications. The killer is not a native."

That didn't fit my other assumptions, but— "Yeah, check those records. You've got the authority."

"I will." Boone smiled. "Now tell me why the mirror wasn't found by the police when they searched for an abandoned message laser."

"What about a mirror in low orbit? Mirrors don't have to be opaque to radar. A plane mirror with the right rotation might give the killer a couple of minutes to pick his shot. And we *know* he was hurried."

Boone snorted. "Ridiculous. An orbiting mirror would have had to be large enough for the killer to see Penzler and vice versa. It would probably have been in sunlight, since the assault took place just before dawn. *Anyone* could have seen it blazing like a beacon."

"All right, it's a stupid suggestion, but it's the best I've got. If we can put a disappearing mirror out there, we've cleared Naomi, haven't we?"

"Absolutely. I think we have enough to get her out of the holding tank *now* pending a second trial."

"Get together with the Mayor," I told him. "I expect he's inclined to be reasonable."

"Good." Boone went back to eating. He had nearly finished that huge plate.

I said, "A mirror can be a thin film stretched on a frame, can't it? If the killer was a lunie cop, he could just pull it apart and stash it. Penzler said three hundred to four hundred meters from his window, but the mirror would be only half that far ... hey. That tilted rock was a hundred and ninety meters away. And everyone else would be searching in the wrong place."

"Tilted rock?"

"Futz, yes! There's a big boulder out there a hundred and ninety meters from his window. Chris thought he was looking past it, but he couldn't say which side. The mirror was probably propped on the rock!"

Boone's deep-set eyes seemed to withdraw further. He ate steadily while he thought. Then, "Very good. Did you have a particular suspect in mind?"

I knew of a policewoman who had been involved in yesterday's search for Chris Penzler. I knew she had a liking for flatlanders. In her love affairs (plural or singular?) she was possessive in a fashion more typical of lunie than flatland custom. She might have involved herself with Chris Penzler, then been rejected by him, at least by her own standards.

She was thoroughly familiar with the Hovestraydt City computer, from age ten. If Naomi could have taken a message laser without leaving a record, why not Laura Drury? She could get into an empty apartment the same way.

A lunie cop could have committed the later, successful

murder. The moon was swarming with them. The killer could have joined the swarm. . .before or after the murder, given that we didn't have an exact time of death.

But. Laura had been at the desk the night Penzler was shot in his bath. Hadn't she? When had she come on duty? Would she have had time to go outside for a folding mirror? The killer had been in a hurry that night. . .

"Hamilton?"

"Sorry. Yeah, I've got suspects, but I still don't have a disappearing mirror."

"This isn't courtroom."

"I know. Keep thinking about the mirror. I'm not a lunie; I'm handicapped."

I returned to my room after the afternoon session.

Outside my window the dreadful alien light of lunar noon was somewhat softened by filter elements in the window. It was still too bright. I tried commands on the window until I got it dimmed a bit.

By now I could have picked out the tilted rock while blind drunk. A hundred and ninety yards away. . . Chris had seen a human figure three to four hundred meters away, past the tilted rock. I looked out at the tilted rock and tried to recall the darkness of a week ago, when Chris Penzler had glimpsed. . .what?

An image in a mirror?

The distances were close enough. One hundred and ninety meters to a mirror on the tilted rock, another hundred and ninety back. Chris had said three to four hundred meters. More reason to think he'd seen a lunie. A lunie, taller than the Belters Penzler was used to, would seem closer.

He'd gone out to look at the tilted rock. Had he found what he was after, before someone had found him? Probably not; he'd left us only a puzzle written in frozen blood.

Alan Watson and I hadn't found much either. . .

My phone was calling me.

It was Boone. "The court has ordered the lady revived,"

he told me. "She's already out. She'll be returned to Hove-straydt City around noon tomorrow. I was told she would need to recuperate overnight in the Copernicus hospital."

Why? But she was out; that was what counted. "Is she awake now?"

"Yes, I've talked to her."

"Okay, I'll—"

"Please don't call her, Hamilton. She sounded tired. She wouldn't give me visual."

"Um. Okay. What's the situation with apartments?"

Boone looked cautiously triumphant. "There's some inconsistency in the records. Mrs. Mitchison was given a room on the second floor because the computer registered all ground floor rooms as occupied. I got a printout of the occupants as of that date. The computer does not list room oh-forty-seven as empty *or* occupied."

"Have you tried to look in oh-forty-seven?"

"Not yet. I'll need a court order."

"No you won't. Have Naomi ask for that room. If anyone flinches, it may tell us something."

He smirked an unLincolnesque smirk. "I like it."

"Okay, Now *tell* somebody about this, will you? Get the judge in charge of reviewing Naomi's conviction and tell him about that disappearing room. Or tell anyone at all."

"Surely you're being overdramatic?"

"You know too much to be safe. We're dealing with someone who can control the lock on your apartment. Look, do it just to make me happy."

"All right, Mr. Hamilton." Smiling, he called off.

I went back to the window.

A mirror would reflect a laser beam for only an instant. No mirror is perfectly reflective, of course. In the first instant of a laser burst the face of a mirror would already be vaporizing. . .going concave, defocussing the beam. . .and it *had* defocussed in mid-burn!

But where had the mirror gone?

The case was loaded with traditional elements. Locked room, inverted, with the failed murderer locked out on the

Moon. Cryptic dying message. Now I was looking for mirror tricks. What next? Disappearing daggers of memory plastic; broken clocks giving spurious alibis—

The moonscape blazed at me through the window. I rubbed my fingers together, remembering...

Alan was on top of the tilted rock, finding nothing. I'd scraped at the shadowed back of the rock with my gloves. White stuff had come off. I'd watched it disappear from my fingertips.

Frost, of course. Water ice. But on the surface of the Moon? It had startled me then. Now, suddenly, it made sense.

And now, suddenly, I had half of the puzzle solved.

12.

The Traditional Elements

"Phone call, Mr Hamilton. Phone call, Mr.—"

"Oh, futz."

"—milton. Phone call—"

"Chiron, answer phone." I disengaged the strap across my chest and sat up.

"Hello, Gil." The screen was blank, but the voice was Naomi's. She sounded tired. There was none of the jubilation you'd expect of someone raised from death.

"Hello. You going to give me vision?"

"No."

Something like post-operative depression, maybe. "Where are you calling from?"

"Here. Hovestraydt City. They say I'm still under arrest."

Had she arrived early? But my clock said noon. I'd been a long time falling asleep.

"Have you talked to Boone yet? We still have an attempted murder to deal with. We'd like to pin both murders on someone."

"Go ahead."

"Are you under drugs?"

"No, but nothing seems to matter much. Who got me out of the freezer?"

"Mostly Alan Watson," I said, for sweet charity's sake.

"Um."

"Naomi, we know where you were when someone shot Chris Penzler in his bath. Boone and I discussed it over the *Chili* at lunch yesterday."

"Over the. . .oh." She thought it out. Clearly I knew, and didn't trust the phone system. "All right. Now what?"

"You're still a suspect. We'd like to produce an actual killer. But he wasn't outside after his first try at Penzler. We have to explain why; or else we have to show where *you* were at that time. Boone says that's not as bad as it sounds. You should talk to him."

"All right."

"We'd like to see you in your apartment."

"Gil, I'd rather not see anyone." Bitterly, "I was just getting used to the idea of being dead."

"So you're not dead. Now what?"

"I don't know."

I couldn't tell her why we had to see the apartment. Not by phone. In her present state, would she take orders? "Call Boone," I said. "Tell him I'll meet him in your apartment. It's oh-forty-seven, isn't it? Tell him to get the police to let us in. Then order us breakfast. Plenty of coffee."

There were several seconds of dead air. Then for the first time I heard emotion in her voice. "All right, Gil," she purred, and was gone.

Bitter satisfaction, that was what it sounded like. But why?

The lunie cop guarding room 047 was a stranger. I had to nerve myself to turn my back on him. Paranoia...

Naomi ushered me in.

Boone was already there, seated at the breakfast table. I didn't understand why he watched me so intently. I was concentrating on what I had to say, not on what I was seeing.

But it seemed to me that my eyes blurred when I looked at Naomi. She seemed distorted, somehow.

She had recovered some of her self-possession, I thought. But she seemed clumsy, and she moved with care. I'd thought she was used to lunar gravity. She said, "Surprise."

And then I saw.

"When you're in the holding tanks, they're not supposed to touch you except in emergencies," she said. "Did you know that?"

I had trouble getting my breath. "I knew it. We've been discussing it in the Conference. What do lunies consider an emergency?"

"Aye, there's the rub," said Naomi. "They apologised, of course. They did the best they could. Seems a Brazilian planetologist waded into a dust pool near Copernicus. It's a wonder she got out at all, with her legs frozen solid. She managed to fall and rip her suit too. Vacuum ruptured both eardrums and one lung and an eye, and the fall broke two ribs. Guess who happened to have the right rejection spectrum to help her out?"

Her legs weren't bad, but they didn't look quite right. Her face didn't look quite right either. And something about her body ... maybe the way she carried herself ...

"She's famous, I gather, this Mary de Santa Rita Lisboa. All hell would break loose if she couldn't get adequate medical treatment at Copernicus. Terrible publicity. For God's sake tell me how I look!"

"Just about the same," I said. It was true. She seemed just faintly distorted. Surgery on her inner ears, twice, had changed the outline of her face. Her eyes weren't quite the same color; how could I have missed that? Her torso seemed twisted. She'd cure that when she learned to walk again. After all, her legs were changed too. They were too thin ... not lunie legs, thank God; she'd have looked like a stork. They'd probably come off a Belter.

Somehow the doctors had found parts that matched, almost. That didn't alter the fact that they had raided a holding tank!

"I'll want you to testify before the Committee," I told her. "I'm going to raise hell."

"Good," she said venomously.

"Boone, did you explain the legal situation?"

Boone nodded. Naomi said, "I wish I'd known all of this before the trial. I don't much like the thought of going through *two* more trials, you know. One to get me clear of this attempted murder charge, one to nail me for having a clone made."

"Will you do it?"

"I suppose so."

I was fighting the abstract horror of knowing that lunie hospitals had been raiding the holding tanks, and a purely personal horror that it could happen to Naomi. Naomi was changed. She wasn't unsightly, just ... changed. Patchwork girl! This was not the woman whose untouchable beauty had sent me fleeing to the asteroid belt long ago.

"Reversing the judgment against you may be more difficult than you think," Boone said. "No judge enjoys ruling that another judge was wrong. We—"

Which reminded me. "Boone? I've found the disappear-ing mirror."

"What? How?"

"Water. You pour a big, flat pan full of water. You freeze it. You take it outside, into vacuum and shadow. Out on the Moon it'll stay at a hundred degrees below zero or less, as long as you keep it in shadow. Now you use the mirror-making facilities to polish it optically flat and silver it. Would it work?"

Boone gaped. It made him look a lot less like Abe Lincoln. He said, "Yes, it'd work. My God, that's why he was in such a hurry! He wanted to kill Penzler just before the sun touched the mirror!"

I smiled. The *eureka* sensation. "But Chris wouldn't coop-erate. He liked playing with the water—"

"When the sun touched the mirror, it would just disap-pear!"

"Almost," I said. "When.it evaporated, some of the water vapor wound up on the back of the tilted rock, in shadow. I found frost there. It'll be gone by now, but we've got other evidence. Harry McCavity says the beam either spread or constricted during the burn. The ice was vaporizing. That's what really saved Chris's life."

I turned to Naomi, who was looking bewildered. "What all of this means is that the murder attempt happened here in this room. Boone, have you had a chance—"

He shook his head. "Nothing odd here at all. These rooms are kept clean by automatics. I expect we won't find any-thing. Gil, the problem is that any citizen of Hovestraydt City could use some corner of the mirror works without being noticed. We even let Boy Scout troops run projects there."

"I know. Too many suspects."

"There ought to be some way to narrow it down—"

"How am I fixed for lawsuits?"

"Nonsense. You're an ARM trying to solve a murder. I'm a lawyer in conference with my client."

"I'd like to know more about Chris's love life," I said. "Naomi—"

"He made a pass at me. Rather crude," she said.

"Would he want to sleep with a lunie woman?"

"That I don't know. Some men like variety. Itch did."

So did I. Futz. So try the phone—

Laura was busy. I got her by belt phone, voice only. "Gil? I couldn't make it last night. I'm short of sleep now. It was the Penzler case."

"No sweat, I was playing detective. I'm playing detective now. Do you know anything about Chris Penzler's taste in women? Even by hearsay?"

"Mmm. Hearsay, maybe. Do you remember the prosecution attorney from Naomi Mitchison's trial?"

The elf woman. Face of cold perfection. "I remember."

"Caroline's fiance got drunk with some friends and was going to go looking for Penzler. They had to talk him out of it. That's all I know. It might have nothing to do with Caroline at all. He wouldn't say."

"Anything else?"

"Nothing I can think of."

"Thanks. When can I call you back?"

"I'm off duty at noon, with luck. But I need sleep, Gil."

"Sometime this evening?"

"Good."

I called off the phone. I thought hard. Then I called the Mayor's office.

"Mr. Hamilton." I wasn't Gil any more, not since yesterday's power play. "You'll find that Naomi Mitchison is out of the holding tank and has been returned here."

"I'm with her now. She's got a few parts missing, did you know that? Missing and replaced."

"I was told," Hove said. "I won't take responsibility for that. I can guess what your attitude will be. Is that why you called?"

"No. Right now I'm more concerned with keeping her out of the holding tank. Hove, you're a politician, you have to deal with all kinds of people. Do you happen to know if Chris Penzler was attracted to lunie women?"

He stiffened a little. "I presume he wouldn't show it. An offworld diplomat wouldn't jeopardize his position in such a fashion."

Was Hove that naive? "We know damn well he offended *somebody*, Hove, and we've got good reason to think it was a citizen of Hovestraydt City. You were here twenty years ago, weren't you? And so was Penzler. Did you hear any rumors then? Were there complaints that had to be settled quietly? Or . . . yeah. Did he make regular trips to the Belt Trading Post, that stopped suddenly?"

"I know the place you mean," Hove said reluctantly. "Aphrodite's. They don't keep records. I can look up records of puffer rentals from twenty years ago, if it's important to you."

"Good. It is."

"Gil, why do you think a local man killed Chris?"

"Nobody else could have made the . . . Mayor, it's too easy to plug into the phone system."

"I'll get you your data," Hove said, and called off.

Boone and Naomi were both looking at me. I said, "If Chris had an affair with a lunie woman, she might be annoyed when he went off with someone else. Lunie customs are funny."

"Flatlander customs are funny," Boone corrected me, "but you may be right. Who?"

"Oh, it's just a possible situation." I got up to pace. I was going to *hate* it if it was Laura. "Here's another. I know a couple of newstapers who might commit a practical joke for kicks and news value. The Belter arrived early; she came to meet our ship. Maybe she had time to make the mirror and place it. She could pass for a lunie. Her torso painting is a naked lady."

"Didn't they actually save Penzler's life?"

"It'd still be a very rough practical joke. Chris might have brought his own enemies from the Belt. Either of the two could know enough programming to steal a message laser."

Boone was nodding. "They're living like a married couple. They must have known each other for some time."

I grinned at him. "They're not lunies, Boone. I just don't know. There are two other Belters on the Committee. They could have had something against him . . ."

Naomi had a thoughtful, puzzled look. I assumed she was confused, not following our line of thought. I hardly noticed when she went to the phone.

"This case does have its traditional elements," I said. "What time is it in Los Angeles?"

"I have no idea," Boone said.

"I should call Luke Garner. He's got a tape library of old mysteries. He'd love this. Dying messages, locked rooms, tricks with mirrors—"

"We don't *have* to produce a killer, you know. That's for the police. Now that we know how the mirror trick was worked, we can clear Mrs. Mitchison."

"Boone, I get edgy when I've solved two-thirds of a puzzle. That's the time when you can get killed."

Naomi tapped at the keys. Hologram head-and-shoulder portraits appeared in a quartered screen. I stepped behind her for a better look. A woman I'd never seen before . . . and Chris Penzler . . . and Mayor Watson . . .

The door announcer said, "Mayor Watson speaking. I'd like to talk to Mr. Hamilton if he's still there. May I come in?"

"Chiron, door open," Naomi said without looking up. Then, "No—"

I looked around as Hove came in. He came in fast. "Close the door," he told Naomi. He was carrying a police message laser.

I went for my gun. ARMs carry a tiny two-shot hand weapon at all times. It fires a cloud of anaesthetic needles.

I'd turned it in on arrival, of course. If that first reflexive move hadn't slowed me, maybe I could have done something.

Boone, half-reclining in a web chair, hadn't had a chance to move at all. Now he raised his hands. So did I.

Naomi said, "I should have thought. I just ... futz!"

The Mayor told her, "Close the door or I'll kill you."

Naomi called the door closed.

"Good enough," Hove said, and he slumped a little. "I'm not sure what to do next. Perhaps you can help me with my problem. If I kill all of you, what are my chances of getting away with it?"

Boone smiled slowly. "Speaking as your lawyer ..."

"Please," said the Mayor. The little glass lens in the end of the gun wavered about, pointing at us all. He could chop us all up before we could do more than twitch. How had he slipped it past the cop? "If you don't speak, I'll kill you. If I catch you in a lie, I'll kill you. Do you understand?"

Boone said, "Consider the political repercussions of three more murders. You'll destroy Hovestraydt City."

I saw it in Hove's face: that shot drew blood. But he said, "You're in a position to convict the *Mayor* of murdering a Belt politician. How would *that* affect the city? I can't allow it. Gil, why did the killer have to be a resident?"

"We're talking about the bathtub attack, remember. Chris saw the killer too close. That makes him tall. It took a resident to borrow the facilities in the mirror works and know how to use them. He also had to futz with the city computer. A lot of residents seem to be good at that." And the mayor, I thought suddenly, would have to be even better.

"So you know about the mirror. Can you tell me how Chris was able to see me? I wasn't fool enough to leave the room lights on while I waited for him to stand up."

"Huh. You weren't?" I thought about it. "Oh. *His* lights were on. You were lighted by the mirror."

He nodded. "That's bothered me ever since. Was it me you suspected?"

"I'm flabbergasted. Hove, *why*?" And then I saw why, out of the corner of my eye, on Naomi's phone screen.

Hove seemed almost disinterested. "Twice he came to the Moon to meddle with our internal affairs. First to impose the holding tanks on us, then to criticize the way we use them. Never mind. Can you think of any way in which the police can trace me? Without your help, of course."

"The guard at the door?"

"He didn't see me. He won't see me leave."

I couldn't think of a thing.

Naomi said, "Mayor, do you see where my finger is now?"

It was on the *Return* key for the phone keyboard. I saw that much, and then I stepped between Naomi and the gun. Hove didn't react fast enough to stop me. "You'll have to shoot through me," I said. "You'll never make it."

Naomi said, "One tap of this key and these four faces appear on every phone screen in the city."

"We can negotiate," I said quickly, soothingly, I hoped. Hove's eyes were going desperate. "You tried to kill Chris Penzler for political reasons? Fine, so say we all. You sliced his hand off six days later? Fine. Do you want to tell us how you managed that?"

He'd been about to fire. Perhaps he still was. "When did it happen?" he asked.

"Chris could have died any time in a five hour period. You can't possibly have an alibi. You must have posed as a policeman. The computer would have issued you a police skintight suit and lost the records."

"Yes. Certainly."

"And Chris left a dying message that points toward you."

I saw the intensity setting on the laser start to unwind, and saw Hove thumb it back to maximum. Hove said, "Did he. Did he really. That's very interesting."

"It points toward you," I said, "but not directly. Chris was only three feet away when the laser sliced his hand off. He must have seen his killer's face, and his chest symbol too.

Why didn't he just write T R E E , or M A Y O R ? Somebody's bound to wonder. Of course, if you just turn yourself in, the case is solved."

Hove seemed lost in thought. Then, "Gil, do you understand what this affair *could* do to my city?"

"It's bad now. It could get much worse, if things run their course."

"Yes. God, yes." He drew himself up, and looking down on us from a great height, he said, "Here are my terms. I want an hour to escape. After that you can tell the police *all that we've discussed.* Agreed? Your word of honor?"

"Yes," I said.

"Yes," said Boone.

Naomi hesitated for several nerve-shattering seconds. Her hand was starting to tremble where she held it poised above the *Return* key. She said, "Yes."

"That on the screen goes back into storage."

"Yes," said Naomi.

"Open the door," the Mayor said.

The laser was under his coat as he stepped into the hall. Naomi called the door closed. Then she said, "Well?"

I mopped away sweat with a napkin. "*My* word of honor is good."

Boone, faintly smiling, was looking at his watch.

"And so say we all," Naomi said. "The bastard! Where will he go?"

"Someplace where he can't be questioned," I said. "He'll get a puffer and go till he's out of air, then find a dust pool."

"You think so?" She looked at the hologram portraits. Four of them. Chris Penzler, and Mayor Hovestraydt Watson, and Alan Watson, and a very tall, elvishly beautiful young woman with long, light brown hair. I could guess who she was, from context. Naomi said, "I wonder how she died."

"You think he killed her? Maybe. It hardly matters now."

"Right." Naomi typed rapidly. The screen cleared.

We waited.

13.
Penalties

We found the guard snoring outside Naomi's door. Hove had fired a cloud of soluble anaesthetic crystals into him, from an ARM issue handgun. It was mine. I'd turned it in on arrival; Hove must have persuaded the computer to release it.

Hove ... well, we waited it out, more or less grimly. He had checked out a puffer and gone. We searched the projected moonscape while we could; he probably hid until Watchbird II set. Jefferson's police searched old mines and known cave systems. Nothing. He certainly hadn't reached the Belt Trading Post; the Belters were looking for him too. Jefferson sent men to search the launch head for the Grimalde mass driver...

Their mistake, I think, was in assuming Hove was desperate to live. Hove's problem was to hide a puffer and a corpse: his own. My own theory is that he blew them both to bits by exploding the puffer's fuel and oxygen.

Alan Watson came in late that night, looking used up. He came back to life when he saw Naomi. They talked seriously for awhile, and then she went off under his long arm. I didn't see them again until next morning.

By then I had talked to Harry McCavity again.

Alan and Naomi were eating a huge breakfast together on the dining level. I managed to be at the buffet when Alan went for more coffee.

"I have to see you in private," I said.

Coffee sloshed. I startled him, I think. He asked, "Isn't it over yet?"

"Mostly it's about you and your father."

A momentary wariness showed in his face. Then, "All right."

I ate breakfast while I waited. Presently Naomi left and Alan came to join me. "She told me about yesterday," he said. "He could have killed you all. I wish none of it had happened."

"So do I. Alan, you're leaving the Moon."

His mouth opened. He stared. "What?"

"Come on, you're not that surprised. I made some promises to Mayor Hove, but I made them at gunpoint. Be off the
Moon within a week. Don't ever come back. Or I'll break
those promises."

He studied my eyes. No, he wasn't that surprised. "You'll
have to spell it out for me."

"I'm not enjoying this," I said. "I'll try to keep it short.
Chris Penzler was close enough to get a good look at the

man who killed him. We know it was a lunie. Even if Penzler didn't know his name, he could have tried to describe the chest emblem. Instead, he left a reference to the attempt to kill him in his bathtub a week earlier. Why would he protect the man who murdered him?"

"Well?"

"You're his son. Naomi finally saw it, and I should have. You're Hove Watson's height, and I took that for genes, but it isn't. You were raised in lunar gravity. Otherwise you look a lot like Chris Penzler and somewhat like your mother and not at all like Hove Watson."

Alan was looking down into his coffee. He was quite pale. "This is all pure speculation, isn't it?"

"It's the kind of speculation that could finish Hovestraydt City, I think. You're supposed to be the Mayor's son, the heir apparent. It's bad enough if Hove killed Penzler for political reasons—"

"I know. You could be right."

"Anyway, I did a little more speculating. Then last night I got Harry McCavity out of bed and made him check a certain pressure suit helmet for traces of dried blood."

Alan looked up. I might have stepped out of a nightmare, the way he looked at me. I said, "What did he do, offer to legitimize you?"

"Offer?" Alan laughed out loud, an ugly sound, then looked quickly around him. Faces had turned. Alan lowered his voice. "He insisted! He was going to name me as his heir and bastard!"

"Did you kill him to get Naomi off the hook?"

"No, no. I wouldn't have hurt him at all if I'd had time to *think*. I could have explained it to him, couldn't I? He just didn't know what he'd be doing to me.

"He said he was my father. He said he was going to *announce* it. He wouldn't listen. And I was holding the laser. I lost my head. It was all over in a thousandth of a second. I sliced his hand off, and he pointed at me and sprayed blood in my face. Blinded me. When I wiped it off the glass he was gone. I looked for him, to get his suit sealed and get him to a hospital. When I found him he was dead."

"Uh huh."

Alan was very pale. He wasn't seeing me at all. He said, "His wrist was still bubbling."

I said, "You could blame Chris for letting his gonads lead him around. You could blame Hove for trying to kill him. It didn't work, but that's what started Chris thinking about his children. Sure you're bound to blame yourself, but, Alan, it wasn't all your fault."

"All right. Now what?"

"If the truth came out, Hell wouldn't hold the political repercussions, and you'd be broken up for parts. I don't want that. But I won't have you in a position of political power, and there's no way you can stay on the Moon without becoming Mayor. Get off the Moon within a week or I'll start talking."

"I suppose you left a letter somewhere, in case something happens to you?"

"Get stuffed."

He stared. "But you're giving me a week to kill you!"

I got up. "You're not the type. And I meant it. I meant it all," I said, and left.

The rules the Committee laid down during the following week included provision for periodic review of lunar legal practice. None of the delegates were especially happy with the new laws. The lunies liked it least; but how could they object, after Naomi's testimony? They compromised.

We were wrapping up the Conference the day Alan Watson left for Ceres. I'd have preferred to see him go, but it didn't matter. Given who he was, he got a police escort. He was definitely gone.

Laura told me about it that evening. "Naomi Mitchison went with him," she said.

"Good."

"Do you mean that?"

"Sure. I like to keep things tidy."

Naomi had asked for her Belt citizenship a few days ago, and Hildegarde Quifting was glad to ram it through for her. Naomi would be an embarrassment on Earth or on the Moon. Moving her to the Belt let everyone breathe easier.

Including Naomi. Old friends on Earth could remember her as she used to be. She needn't stand trial for illegal cloning. Her little girl would be waiting for her.

She might even be in love with Alan Watson. Futz, I even like the idea. Let it stand.